How Many Days Until Tomorrow?

Written by Caroline Janover

Illustrated by Charlotte Fremaux

Woodbine House   2000

Cover and interior illustrations by: Charlotte M. Fremaux

Library of Congress Cataloging-in-Publication Data

Janover, Caroline.
    How many days until tomorrow? / by Caroline Janover.
        p. cm.
    Sequel to: Josh, a boy with dyslexia.
    Summary: Josh, who has dyslexia, spends the summer on an island off the coast of Maine and finds that he has much to prove to his gruff grandfather and his older brother.
    ISBN 1-890627-22-4 (pbk.)
    [Dyslexia—Fiction. 2. Grandfathers—Fiction. 3. Brothers—Fiction. 4. Islands—Fiction. 5. Maine—Fiction.] I. Title.

PZ7.J2445 Ho 2000
[Fic]—dc21   00-060015

Manufactured in the United States of America

10 9 8 7 6 5 4 3 2 1

To my father

and

to all my brothers

and sisters

who for years

have skipped rocks

(never off the dock)

from the shores

of our island

in Maine

1.

Josh knew his mother was crying. She stood alone on the dock and blew her nose into a tissue. Waving her red bandanna in the stiff, cold wind, she yelled across the water, "Have fun!"

"How can I possibly have fun?" Josh muttered under his breath. He could barely hear his mother's voice over the putt-putt sound of the lobster boat's engine. Spending a month on an island in Maine with his teasing older brother and grandparents he hardly knew was not his idea of a good time. He wanted to stay home in New Jersey, play All Star baseball, and hang out with his friends.

Josh stood up and waved with both arms.

"Sit down!" his grandfather shouted over the roar of the engine. The boat hit a swell. Josh felt the icy salt spray of the wave on his cheek. He wondered if he'd

1

get seasick. Once he had visited a cruise ship in New York Harbor. He'd felt seasick even though the boat was still tied up to the pier. "Can I ride in the front of the boat?" Josh yelled to his grandfather.

"Stay where you are," his grandfather barked without taking his eyes off the blackening horizon.

"Don't you know the front of a boat is called the bow?" Simon shouted. Simon was thirteen. Just because

he was in the Gifted and Talented Program in school, his brother thought he knew everything. Josh had one aim in life. That aim was to do something, anything, better than his brother.

Josh snapped up the front of his yellow rain slicker. He was glad his mother had forced him to wear his NY Jets sweatshirt. He shivered as the boat plunged up and down in the choppy waves.

3

Josh glanced at his grandmother to see if she looked worried. She sat in a worn, yellow rain slicker on the opposite side of the boat, surrounded by canvas bags full of groceries. A seagull skimmed across the water. It flew into the wind with a flapping fish in its beak. "He's having the same dinner we are!" Nana cried cheerfully.

Josh felt knots in his stomach. He hated fish. He hugged his arms around his chest as his teeth began to chatter. Looking through the motor's smelly exhaust, he could no longer see his mother standing on the dock in Moxie Cove. She was probably already driving back to New Jersey. She was in a warm car. She could stop at a restaurant and order anything she wanted for supper, like a double cheeseburger and french fries.

"How much longer 'til we get to the island?" Josh called to his grandmother.

"Don't you remember? Seal Island is four miles out to sea," Simon yelled back. "Mom says it takes thirty minutes to get there."

"So how much longer?" Josh cried.

His grandmother cupped her hand over her eyes. Josh noticed that she had green paint underneath her fingernails. Her wide, square face looked like his mom's face but with more lines around her eyes and mouth. Her saggy skin was as wrinkled as tissue paper.

"Cranberry Island is off to port," she said. "In this wind, the island must be another twenty minutes out to sea."

Josh saw raindrops smacking the water. Lightning zigzagged in the distance across the black sky.

"Looks like a thunder squall," Gramps yelled. "Cover the suitcases and groceries." He threw a large plastic bundle into his wife's lap. With a fierce look, he bent over the steering wheel and pointed the bow of the *Odyssey* directly into the wind. "If I go full throttle, we can race the storm to the island."

Josh felt his heart thumping. Lightning was attracted to metal and water. The lobster boat had a metal motor and it was the only boat in Muscongus Bay. Dodging brightly colored lobster buoys, his grandfather steered the boat head-on into the storm.

As they lurched up and down in the choppy sea, salty spray blew over the bow and hit Josh in the face. Seawater splashed up onto the wooden seats. Josh wondered how a man as frail and bony as his grandfather could keep control of the boat. His sunken cheeks and lizard skin made him look over one hundred years old.

Simon threw the plastic tarp over the straw basket full of clean laundry. The fresh sheets on top were already damp. Josh could think of nothing worse. After a fish dinner, he'd have to sleep in soggy, wet sheets. At least it was Sunday night. He and Simon could curl up in a warm quilt and watch *Emergency Squad* on Channel 7.

Suddenly Josh's heart sank. How could he forget? He couldn't watch TV, not tonight or any night, not for one whole month. The house on Seal Island had no electricity! He'd have to lie in wet sheets and read by candlelight. Josh hated to read. Simon had packed sixteen books. Josh had only packed one book, the one the teachers force you to read before you start the sixth grade in middle school.

"You okay, Rosie?" Gramps called. He was a tall man with stooped shoulders and bushy eyebrows as thick as toothbrushes.

"Of course I'm okay," Nana called back, clinging to the laundry basket. She tightened the wet bandanna over the white braid wrapped around her head. The bandanna looked just like the one his mom had waved on the Moxie Cove dock.

The ocean swells made Josh feel hot waves of seasickness. Even Simon looked miserable. His lips turned the color of plums. He held his L.L. Bean backpack full of precious summer reading tightly between his knees. Goosebumps stood out on his long, hairy legs.

"How much longer?" Josh called to his grandmother.

"Not long now. The shack over there on Fog Island burned to the ground last summer," she said, pointing to a pile of burnt timbers.

"How come?" Simon yelled from the other side of the boat.

"Could have been lightning . . . could have been teenagers . . . no one really knows."

"What's wrong, Josh?" Simon called. "You're white as a ghost."

"I think I'm going to throw up," Josh cried, standing up.

"SIT DOWN!" yelled his grandfather. "Didn't I tell you to stay seated? When the captain gives an order, it is meant to be followed."

"Sorry," said Josh, sinking into a puddle of water on the wooden bench. He watched a spray of lightning crackle across the sky as thunder boomed even louder. If only he were sitting next to his mother in a warm car driving back to New Jersey. Just because his parents were going to England for business and vacation didn't mean he had to be sent to Maine against his will.

Josh shivered and bent his head between his legs, afraid he might puke or faint. If he passed out in the lobster boat, he wondered if his bug-eyed grandfather would take him back to the dock in Moxie Cove.

2.

The wind slapped Josh's face with stinging rain. Water trickled down the back of his neck. Giant white swells broke over the bow of the boat. Pounding up and down, Josh felt like he was on the bucking bronco machine at the mall. He wondered why his grandfather didn't have the sense to turn back to the mainland. Couldn't he see that the lives of his two grandsons were in danger?

"Look off to starboard." His grandmother turned her short, plump body on the seat and pointed. "I see the island!"

Josh sat up straight and looked to the left. He saw miles of ocean lit up by dancing threads of lightning. There was no land in sight.

"Look the other way, Bro!" Simon shouted, pointing to the right.

Josh wished that he had a microscope or a telescope, the one that made things look bigger from far away. Through the downpour, he saw an island in the shape of a new moon. It had a large meadow and a beach on one end and a pine forest and rock cliffs on the other end. In the middle of the island stood one lone house with a red door and two chimneys. A tattered American flag whipped in the wind by the dock.

The sight of the tiny house and the roll and pitch of the waves made Josh feel even sicker. When he felt woozy at home, his Mom or Dad would bring him fizzy ginger ale and let him watch TV. There was no TV or ginger ale or loving parents on this island.

Gramps slowed the boat as they approached the entrance of the harbor. The pounding rain began to soften into a cold drizzle.

"Think the tide is high enough, Rosie?"

"Certainly hope so." Nana stood up stiffly and pushed strands of wet, white hair off her face.

"What happens if it's not?" Simon asked anxiously.

"We unload at the drain tide dock when the tide gets too low for the big dock." Nana pointed at a pile of rocks covered with green seaweed and floating brown kelp just below the water's surface.

"You mean we'd have to get our feet wet?" Josh asked.

"Your feet are sopping wet already, dummy," said his brother.

Gramps steered the boat past the drain tide dock and pulled up alongside the big dock. It was built with giant, flat rocks and millions of stones and pebbles. Huge logs the size of telephone poles held the dock together. "Grab the painter," Gramps instructed in a hoarse voice.

"What painter?" asked Simon.

"The rope!" His grandfather pointed a hairy finger at a coil of rope on the bow of the boat. "Don't you boys know anything about boats? You, get up and climb the ladder."

"Who, me?" Josh stood up and stepped toward the wooden ladder. His blue jeans were so wet it felt like he was dragging his legs under water. He climbed the ladder straight up the side of the dock.

"Throw the painter to your brother," Gramps yelled to Simon over the drone of the engine.

Simon heaved the rope up to Josh. The rope went up about six feet, but not high enough for Josh to catch it. Josh leaned over the side of the dock. "Throw it up again," he yelled.

"Tie a clove hitch over the post," Gramps shouted, putting the boat's engine in reverse.

Josh grabbed the dripping rope. "What's a hitcher clove?"

With a disgusted grunt, his grandfather climbed stiffly up the ladder and knotted the rope to the dock post himself. Josh didn't remember his grandfather being so ornery. When he and Nana had come to New Jersey for Christmas three years ago, he'd given him $15.00 in cash to buy a present. He'd carved a bird out of wood as a present for his parents. Back in New Jersey, Gramps had seemed nice. Since they'd gotten to Maine, he hadn't smiled once.

Nana stood up. "Now you handsome young men can help us unload the supplies," she said in a chirpy voice, pointing to the basket full of clean laundry. Josh watched his grandmother pull her plump body up the steep ladder steps. Her ankles were swollen the size of melons. As she crawled onto the dock, she panted, "After Hobson turns on the water pump, I'll make hot soup to warm us up. My clam chowder was featured in the church cookbook!"

"How come you don't wash clothes on the island?" Simon asked, hoisting the heavy laundry basket up to Josh.

"Not enough fresh water. Some years our well runs dry by August. If that happens, God forbid, your grandfather has to bring bottled water out from the mainland."

"Does that mean I can't take hot showers?" Simon groaned. Ever since he'd started dating girls, he showered for fifteen minutes every morning. He wore lemon after shave lotion even though he didn't have any whiskers, only brown fuzz.

"You can bathe in the tidal pool Hobs built for your mother and Rachel. By the way," Nana added, "never flush the toilet unless it is absolutely necessary. As we used to say to the girls: 'If it's yellow, let it mellow. If it's brown, flush it down!'"

At least they have a toilet, Josh thought. Once he'd visited a friend in upstate New York. You had to go in the woods where there were bees and poison ivy and no toilet paper.

The thunderstorm rumbled farther out to sea. The sky over the mainland was turning pink. Gramps pushed the wheelbarrow full of groceries along a thin wooden plank in the middle of the rocky dock.

Josh dragged his soggy suitcase along the bumpy pebbles. He picked up a flat rock ringed with a white stripe. With his wrist, he flicked the rock off the dock so that it skipped along the water.

Gramps spun around, hearing the splash. "Never, EVER do that again!"

"What? What did I do?" Josh asked innocently.

"Never throw rocks off this dock. Who do you think carried all those stones up here bucket after bucket after bucket?"

"Sorry," muttered Josh.

With a grunt, Gramps continued to push the heavy wheelbarrow up the grass path to the house.

Josh and Simon made three trips up and down the wet path from the dock to the house. They carried the suitcases, canvas bags of groceries, the laundry basket, two propane gas tanks, pots of lilies for the garden, and a box of cedar shingles to patch the leaking roof.

Nana carried a basket of fresh vegetables from her garden at the winter house in Moxie Cove. She tucked painting canvas wrapped in plastic bubble wrap under her arm. Josh knew that his grandmother was an artist. In New Jersey, a watercolor she had painted of the house on Seal Island hung above the fireplace. In the painting, the old stone house looked big and pretty. In real life, the house looked cramped and ugly. One window shutter was hanging off and the weathered shingles on the workshop looked rotten. The front door was covered with peeling chips of red paint. The thought of his three story, air-conditioned home in New Jersey made Josh feel even sadder. He swallowed hard and tried to wiggle numb toes in his wet sneakers. At least they had made it alive to dry land.

3.

Josh lifted his suitcase onto the lumpy bed in the attic. Simon had grabbed the best bed. It was next to the window with a view of the harbor. On the wax-stained table between the two beds there were four new candles and a basket of seashells. Josh pulled back the patchwork quilt. Clean, dry sheets were neatly tucked into the sagging, horsehair mattress. He quickly changed into dry clothes, dropped his soggy blue jeans on the floor, and shoved his suitcase underneath the bed.

Simon unpacked his suitcase. He arranged his socks, underpants, shorts, jeans, and shirts in neat piles in the bureau next to the rusted iron baby's crib. After hanging his wet clothes over a rafter to dry, he unpacked his comb and toothbrush. "How can I part my hair without a decent mirror?" he groaned.

"Check out the so-called bathroom," Josh suggested. At the other end of the long, narrow attic there was a toilet and a sink behind a wooden screen. A tiny window covered with cobwebs let in dim shafts of sunlight.

"I can't see a thing!" Squinting in front of the mirror above the sink, Simon sneezed violently. "I'm allergic!" he cried, pointing to bunches of dried flowers hanging from the rafters on a row of nails.

"Don't panic," said Josh. Balancing on top of an old trunk, he pulled down the flowers and stuffed them into Simon's empty suitcase. "You'll be safe now," he said.

"Thanks, Bro," said Simon, forcing a smile. "This place is a dump!"

"You can say that again. I'm going to check out the first floor."

While Simon arranged his books in alphabetical order, Josh felt his way down the steep, creaking attic stairs. He peeked into his grandparents' bedroom. Nana's bureau was cluttered with photos of her two daughters, five grandchildren, friends, and family dogs. On his grandfather's bureau there was a silver hairbrush, a photo of an old lady in a black dress, and a clamshell full of pennies. Nana's knitting yarns filled a large basket by the door to the bathroom. A mildewed

17

shower curtain hid a tiny stall next to the unflushed toilet. Bottles of perfume, body lotion, sunscreen, and lipsticks were lined neatly along the window sill. In a glass on the sink, Josh noticed two worn toothbrushes and a collection of bird feathers.

In the living room, books crammed a wobbly shelf that stretched from floor to ceiling. Josh examined a dusty, wooden model of a Friendship Sloop propped next to a stack of books about sailing. A painting of Seal Island Harbor hung above the fireplace. A tiny bird's nest with a blue egg, a basket of beach glass, and a perfect orange crab shell sat on the window sill. Josh tapped a key on the upright piano. It sounded muffled and flat. Simon could play Mozart and boogie rap on the piano. Josh had quit music lessons in the third grade.

Josh walked through the dining room and into the kitchen. Nana stood in a wrinkled blue dress, stirring the clam chowder. She was wearing red lipstick and white powder on her sagging cheeks. Josh noticed red polish neatly painted on each toenail of her swollen feet. She smelled of the same sweet perfume his mother wore to work.

"I'll set the table," Josh said, grabbing a bunch of spoons and forks from a wooden box on the kitchen counter.

"That would be helpful, dearie. Your grandfather made me that silverware box for our first wedding anniversary," she said proudly.

"That's cool," said Josh.

"This year he rebuilt the back porch for our forty-seventh anniversary. Hobs is as nimble as a squirrel after his hip replacement. Before the operation the pain was so fierce he could barely walk. All day he sat and pecked at his typewriter. It hurt too much to move around."

"Gramps got a new hip?" Josh asked as he reached for the plates.

"Your Aunt Rachel had to drive him all the way to Boston for the operation. Funny to think of your grandfather hinged together with plastic joints."

Josh watched carefully as his grandfather walked into the kitchen. He hardly had a limp. He was still wearing tall rubber boots and his yellow rain slicker. Wet strands of gray hair stuck to his forehead. His scruffy whiskers were the same color as his bushy eyebrows. His bulging, blood-shot eyes looked as if they'd been boiled.

"Besides fish and chowder, what are we eating for supper?" Josh asked. "I'm starving."

Josh felt a hand clamp down on his shoulder. His grandfather was over six feet tall, but stooped and frail looking except for his giant hands. His hands were thick and hairy and covered with brown spots from years of lobstering in the sun.

"You are NOT starving, Joshua," he announced.

"But I haven't eaten a thing since we had lunch at Burger King."

"Hungry, perhaps, but starved you are not. English is a rich language. We must use it properly."

"Okay, Gramps," said Josh, looking down at his wet sneakers.

"My name is Grandfather, not Gramps." He opened a cupboard and took out a bottle. Pouring whiskey into a glass, he swirled three ice cubes with his hairy finger.

Nana interrupted in a bubbly voice, "What a treat to finally get you boys out to the island! I've been after your mother for years to send you for a good long visit."

Josh smiled weakly and carried two milk glasses into the dining room. He watched his grandfather gulp down a swig of whiskey. His nose was so long it stuck out like a beak between his bulging eyes. Gramps set his drink on the fireplace mantle. With a grunt, he bent down and stacked three logs on a bed of crumpled newspaper and dry kindling sticks.

Josh walked back into the kitchen. "In health class the school nurse said that alcohol kills off brain cells," he whispered. "Does Gramps drink straight whiskey every night?"

Nana slowly stirred the chowder. "Hobs drinks to dull the pain," she answered softly.

4.

Grandfather struck a wooden match and lit the crumpled newspaper in the fireplace. The sticks crackled as the kindling burst into leaping flames. Taking another sip of whiskey, Gramps announced, "First rule of island living, boys, never leave a room without first putting up the fire screen."

"How could firemen get out here?" Simon called from the living room. He had curled up in a chair with a soggy paperback.

"Precisely the point, my boy. They can't." Without another word, Gramps took his drink and left the room.

Josh finished setting the table and lit the candles on either side of the fruit bowl. He bent over to rock the wooden cradle next to the fireplace. In the cradle there was a rag doll. It was tucked under a pink blanket covered with moth holes. A driftwood mobile hung over the doll's head. It was made out of dangling feathers, twigs, and seashells.

"Your mother slept in that cradle." Nana said, carrying bowls of clam chowder to the table. "We bought the island from a fisherman the year before your mother was born. Hobson had summers off from teaching at the university. He took up lobstering to pay the bills."

"What do you do out here all summer?" Josh asked.

"Hobs lobstered for close to thirty years. Before his hip gave out, he'd be out there pulling traps in all kinds of weather. He stopped hauling, I'd say, about the time he got let go from the university."

"Don't you get lonely out here, Nana?" Josh asked.

"I've got my piano and paints to keep me busy." Josh sensed a core of sadness in his grandmother's eyes. "Now go call your brother and Hobson to the table." Nana untied her apron and hung it on a hook by the stove.

Gramps pulled out Nana's chair. Then he sat down at the head of the table and pulled a cloth napkin out of the silver napkin ring. He had combed his salt and pepper gray hair and changed into a tweed jacket with leather patches on the elbows. "I understand you are interested in history," he said to Simon. "Your mother tells me that you are an avid reader."

"I'm a history buff all right, especially when it comes to the Civil War," Simon said, cracking his knuckles.

Josh sat down at the table. "I'm into baseball."

"I beg your pardon."

"Me and my pals . . . "

"My pals and I," Grandfather corrected.

"My pals and I are all into baseball," said Josh. "Last year we almost got first place in the series but

Scooter broke his leg. He broke it skateboarding. Scooter is our pitcher."

"You cannot be "into" a sport, young man. You can enjoy a sport but it is incorrect to say that you are 'into' it."

"Hobson taught Latin for forty-eight years at the University of Maine," Grandmother said. "He is very precise about language. What do you like to read, Josh?" she added.

Josh hid the codfish under his mashed potatoes. "I'm not really into literature," he replied.

"Josh has dyslexia," Simon explained. "He hates to read."

Josh felt his cheeks getting hot. He jiggled his feet under the table.

"The spelling in your letters is getting much better, dearie," Nana said. She patted Josh's hand and offered him more fish. "I hope you're not a pick and nibble eater like your dad."

Gramps took another swig of whiskey. "Dyslexia does not originate from my side of the family." He wiped his pencil-thin lips with a corner of his napkin. "We are all excellent spellers."

"So you speak Latin?" Josh asked, trying to change the subject.

"One does not SPEAK Latin. One reads Latin."

Simon burst into giggles. "Josh is such a dolt! He doesn't even know that you don't speak Latin."

Josh sat in cold silence as Simon bragged on to his grandparents about how great he was in school. He told about making the high honor roll and being voted eighth grade class treasurer. Gramps looked impressed. Once he even smiled.

Wishing his brother would gag on a codfish bone, Josh poked at his lima beans. If he ever got a good grade in school, it was pure luck. Even when he studied for hours, he'd mess up on tests. Simon would go to Harvard like his dad. Josh imagined he'd end up fixing car engines or selling movie tickets at the mall. School was not his thing. The thought of starting sixth grade already made his stomach do flip flops.

Nana glanced at Josh anxiously, twisting the pearl necklace around her fingers. "My, you've grown so tall and handsome!" she cried. "Simon, be a lamb and clear the table."

"Okey-dokey," said Simon, cracking his knuckles. "I always aim to please."

"I'll do it!" Josh jumped up from the table. He stacked the dinner plates on the fish platter. In the kitchen, he turned on the sink faucet. A stream of water washed over the soup bowls.

"STOP! STOP! You're wasting water!" Gramps stood up stiffly and marched into the kitchen. "I do the dishes in this house," he announced, pushing Josh away from the sink.

"Your grandfather is a great help," Nana cried in a fake, cheerful voice.

If it hadn't been for the homemade blueberry pie on the counter, Josh would have run upstairs to the attic and gone to bed.

5.

Josh woke up in the night. He had to go to the bathroom. He climbed out from under the warm quilt and felt his way in the dark along the attic wall.

"Ouch!" he cried out.

"What's wrong?" Simon sat up in bed. "Where are you?"

"I broke my toe," Josh moaned. "I can't find the bathroom."

"Stay where you are." Simon pulled the Boy Scout flashlight out from under his pillow. He searched the attic with the thin beam of light until he spotted Josh sitting on the floor. "You okay?"

"I stubbed my toe on that stupid trunk," Josh said, rubbing his foot. "It kills."

"You'll live," said Simon. He sneezed and turned off the flashlight.

"But I can't see!" Josh cried. "I'm going to pee in my pajamas."

Simon pointed a ray of light toward the bathroom. "Hurry up! These batteries have to last a whole month."

Josh limped toward the toilet. Climbing back under the quilt, he remembered he wasn't supposed to flush. Josh lay in bed and listened to the rain drumming down on the attic roof. Plop, Plop, Plop . . . drips of water hit the bottom of a bucket next to his bed. It sounded like a Chinese water torture. How could his parents have done this to him? All his friends back home were playing Nintendo, skateboarding, diving off the high board, watching action videos, and going to the movies with girls. He was trapped on a boring island with a leaking roof and a brother who tormented him day and night. He'd begged to spend the month living with his best friend, Zipper. He'd even promised his dad to read a book a day and practice his math facts if he could only stay home in New Jersey.

After a restless sleep, Josh limped down the attic stairs for breakfast. His throbbing big toe looked swollen.

"How did you sleep?" Nana tied an apron around her wide hips. Her wispy, white hair was pulled back into a soft bun.

"Okay, I guess, but in the night I stubbed my toe and the roof leaks and Simon sneezed and sneezed. He's allergic to dust."

"The attic is my favorite room in the house, except for the mice."

"The mice?"

"Field mice nest in the walls." Nana carried two bowls of steaming cereal to the table. "What a shame it's still raining. I just bought a yummy shade of moss green for my oil painting of the pine trees."

Tucking his shirt into his baggy pants, Simon walked into the dining room. "What's that?" he asked, pointing at the cereal.

"Hot oatmeal."

"Don't you have any Froot Loops or Apple Jacks?" Simon asked.

Nana shook her head. "Hobson only eats oatmeal. I make it every morning except for Sunday. On Sunday we eat blueberry pancakes."

Josh counted on his fingers the number of days until he could get a decent breakfast.

"Your grandfather has a surprise for you in the workshop," Nana said. "He's been working out there since six this morning."

Josh felt in no hurry to join his grandfather in the shop. After breakfast he wiped the mugs in the drying rack with a ragged dishtowel. Reaching to put away the cereal bowls, Josh noticed a black box on the top kitchen shelf.

"What's in here?" he asked.

"That's in case of an emergency," Nana explained. "Several years ago your mother insisted we buy one for the island."

"What is it?" Josh asked. "A gun?"

"Heavens no! It's a cellular telephone. I'd love to call the girls and my friends ashore but Hobs says it's not for 'idle chatter,' only emergencies."

"How does it work?" asked Josh, opening the box.

"Just like any other telephone. You dial one and then the area code and number. We used it once when the lobster boat ran aground."

"Don't you listen to the radio?" Josh asked, pointing to a little radio hidden behind a pitcher of dried beach heather.

"Country western is all we get out here. I'd rather listen to the music of the wind and my birds. Hobs and I do turn on the 5:00 o'clock news from time to time."

Simon walked into the kitchen sneezing violently. He was carrying a package. His hair was neatly parted and his

31

breath smelled of mouthwash. "Look what Gramps gave me!" he said. "Mom sent this package for a rainy day."

"Cool," said Josh, peering in the box. "That's a wicked battleship model."

"The battleship is mine," said Simon, sneezing again. "You get the aircraft carrier."

"How come?"

"Because I'm the oldest, that's why! Gramps says we can work on the models in the shop." Simon held his nose to stop another sneeze.

Josh shrugged. He hung the dishtowel on a peg and followed his brother through the little storage room to the workshop. Stopping to examine a rusted birdcage sitting on a shelf next to cans of soup and bags of flour, he said, "Let's call him Grumps instead of Gramps. I've never met such a weirdo in my life."

"I think Gramps is cool!" Simon replied. He picked up a torn butterfly net and swung it through the air like a baseball bat. As Simon unlatched the door to the workshop, Josh felt a sinking wave of loneliness. Even his own brother didn't understand. He took a deep breath and counted to ten. His tutor said to breathe deeply when he felt like swearing, crying, or punching someone in the nose.

"I suppose you boys expect to work in my shop," Gramps muttered, looking up from his workbench. He brushed a handful of wood shavings onto the floor and pointed to an old door resting on two sawhorses. "Sit there," he instructed, pushing two wooden crates under the door. "No room where I'm working."

Josh looked up at the coils of rope and red and yellow lobster buoys hanging from the rafters. The workshop was cluttered with shelves full of paint cans and carpentry tools. Fishing rods, oars, firewood, wooden lobster pots, and broken furniture filled the dimly lit room. The only light in the workshop filtered through cracked window panes covered with salt spray and spider webs the size of pot holders.

"That's wicked cool!" Josh cried. "Gramps, you sure know how to carve real-looking birds."

"That bird is neither wicked nor cool," his grandfather replied. He narrowed his toothbrush eyebrows and scowled at Josh.

"Wicked means good," Simon explained in his brother's defense. Gramps' expression did not change. "We've decided that I get the battleship," Simon continued. "Josh wants the aircraft carrier."

Simon carefully opened the battleship box and began to sort hundreds of plastic pieces according to size, color, and shape. Josh ripped open his box and immediately glued the two sides of the plastic hull together. He didn't even bother to unfold the directions.

"It's not going to come out right, Bro," Simon warned. "Want me to help you read the directions?"

"Directions are stupid. I'll do it my own way."

"Not me!" Simon cracked his knuckles. "I'm making my model come out perfectly."

Josh glued three green plastic airplanes to the flight deck. Catching the chill of his grandfather's stare, he tapped the worktable with his glue stick.

"Stop jiggling the table. This work requires exact precision." Simon picked a tiny plastic piece off the floor.

Josh stopped tapping and began to hum. "Let's bring the radio out here," he said, trying to pretend he was having a good time.

"I find it impossible to concentrate with any type of noise or distraction," Gramps growled in a voice as scratchy as sandpaper.

"Josh is just trying to make conversation," explained Simon.

"If you boys wish to converse, you'll have to take your models elsewhere. I have worked in this shop for over forty-five years with neither a radio nor idle chatter, and that is exactly how I intend to keep it."

"You mean, when in Rome do as the Romans do?"

"Precisely, my boy." Gramps gave Simon a tight smile.

Swinging his legs back and forth under the worktable, Josh thought about all the times he'd put models together with his dad. His dad told stories about the battleships and the wars and what it felt like to fight on the front line. His dad LIKED to talk.

"I'm leaving!" Josh announced in a voice so loud it made Simon jump. Pushing open the heavy workshop door, Josh limped down three stone steps into the foggy morning drizzle.

6.

Josh walked in the misty morning rain to the end of the dock. A lobster boat was pulling up traps just outside the harbor. Seagulls squawked as they circled the boat. The air smelled of wet grass, low tide, and pine trees. Josh suddenly longed for a whiff of New Jersey air pollution. Kicking stones along the dock, he decided not to explore the path into the woods. Without Simon, he was afraid of getting lost.

Josh limped back up the path to the house. He opened the latch on the front door. Smelling something wonderful, he walked into the kitchen. Quickly, he stuffed two warm oatmeal-raisin cookies in his mouth. Out the kitchen window, Josh could see his grandmother sitting in the field in front of her painting easel. A beach umbrella was stuck into the wet ground to protect her painting from the foggy drizzle.

Josh reached for the black box on the top kitchen shelf. His grandmother had said that the cell phone was to be used only in case of emergency. As far as he was concerned, this was an emergency. He hid the phone under his baggy sweater and ran up the attic stairs. Sitting down on the closed toilet seat cover, he carefully punched one, the area code, and his mother's telephone number at work.

"Could I please speak to Mrs. Grant," he said in a deep voice.

"One moment, please." The operator rang his mother's extension four times. Josh felt his heart pounding.

"International Loan Department, Susan Grant speaking."

"Mom, this is Josh!" His voice cracked. "Mom, you've got to come get me. I can't stand it out here. Simon is being really mean and Gramps hates me. I want to come home."

There was a long pause. Josh could tell that his mother was forcing her voice to stay calm. "I can't do that, Josh," she said. "Your father and I leave for Europe tomorrow night."

"I could come with you!" Josh cried. "I'll stay in the hotel room while you have meetings. I'll even read. I won't be any trouble. I promise!"

"This is not a trip for children," his mother interrupted.

"But I'm not a child! I'm twelve. I'm a preteen! It would be so educational. I could write history reports about kings and queens next year in sixth grade."

"I'm sorry, Josh. You'll just have to make the best of the situation. Father and Mummy aren't so bad once you get to know them."

"Are you kidding? Gramps corrects every other word I say. He thinks I'm a moron!"

"Then talk to your grandmother. She thinks you're wonderful."

"All Nana wants to do is paint pictures of trees. I can't stand it out here. There is NOTHING TO DO!"

"I spent many, many summers on Seal Island, Josh. There is plenty to do! Use your imagination."

"But Mom . . ."

"I've got to go, Josh. I'm late for a meeting."

Josh stood up. "Don't hang up!" he pleaded, pacing back and forth in front of the toilet. "There is something else I haven't told you," he sputtered. "I'm sick! I've been running a high fever since we got here."

"Nana will take good care of you, Josh," his mother said in a thin, shaky voice. "She's just thrilled to have you there."

"That's because she doesn't want to be left alone with her weirdo husband," Josh mumbled. "Besides, I'm probably contagious. Do you want your elderly parents to get really sick?"

"You'll feel better soon. Give everyone my love." Without really saying good-bye, his mother hung up the phone. Josh looked in the cracked bathroom mirror. Stinging tears spilled onto his cheeks. He put a cold washcloth over his face, took a deep breath, and counted to ten. Simon would tease him forever if he knew that he'd been crying.

Josh threw himself down on his unmade bed. He took more deep breaths, only this time he counted to twenty. Reaching for his Yankee Baseball calendar, he crossed off the first day of the month with a red pen. "How many days until tomorrow?" he whispered. When he was a little kid, that was a question he'd asked his mother over and over again. Tears dribbled down his pale cheeks as he stared at the weeks and weeks of empty tomorrows that lay ahead.

Josh blew his nose and picked up his summer reading book. The Resource Program teacher had made him promise to read a half hour a day. He slid his eyes over the first paragraph and threw the book on the floor. Reading small print without proper electric lighting would strain his stinging eyes. He lay on his back, hands behind his head, and began to dream up poison recipes to feed Grumps and Simon. He could stir bird doo doo in their oatmeal or snip pieces of seaweed in their salad....

As Josh stared up at the roof rafters, he heard a scratching sound. It came from behind the trunk he'd tripped over in the night. Josh climbed off the bed and tiptoed closer. A gray mouse scampered across the hooked rug and ran under Simon's bed.

Ever since he'd seen the movie *Stewart Little,* Josh had wanted a pet mouse. He hid the telephone under his sweater and limped down the attic stairs to get the birdcage from the storage room. As he walked through the dining room, Josh heard footsteps. Slipping the telephone under the doll's blanket in the cradle, he held his breath. The latch on the storage room door opened and his grandfather stepped into the dining room.

"Hello, Grandfather," Josh said politely, forcing a smile.

"Where is Rosie?"

"She's out painting the pine tree," Josh said, backing toward the kitchen. He could see the black phone box sitting on the counter next to the oatmeal cookies.

Stroking his prickly whiskers, Grandfather sniffed the air. "Something certainly smells delectable," he said.

"You go find Nana and I'll bring you both some oatmeal cookies." Josh inched his body in front of the kitchen counter.

"Fine idea, young man. You certainly have a talented older brother. He is doing a superb job building that model."

"Simon's real smart," Josh agreed. "Only sometimes he can be a pain in the neck."

"I imagine you annoy your brother as well. It all comes with the territory." Grandfather raised his bushy eyebrows in alarm. "What is that box doing on the counter?"

"Well you see, I had to make a phone call. It...it... it was an emergency. I had to speak to Mom. I want to go home. I mean I think I'm sick." Josh tried to keep his upper lip from quivering.

"You are not a baby, so don't act like one," Grandfather snorted. He shook the empty box. "Where is the cellular telephone?"

Josh pointed to the cradle, afraid to speak.

Grandfather threw the pink baby blanket on the floor. "Never use this phone again. Do I make myself perfectly clear?" he shouted.

"Yes, sir." Josh saw his grandfather's powerful hand swinging toward his face. He winced, then felt the huge hand rest gently on his forehead.

"No fever. There's nothing wrong with you except fear of hard work," he muttered. "I told Rosie. I told Rosie it was a mistake to invite you boys out here."

"I agree! It was a BIG mistake," Josh cried. "Now will you take me and Simon back to the mainland?"

Grandfather ran his tongue over his yellowed teeth and shook his head. "As soon as it stops raining, I want you boys up on the roof. We've got leaks to patch before winter." Grandfather blew his pointed nose in a hankie and walked out the back door.

Josh put the cell phone back on the top shelf. His heart was thumping worse than when he had to read out loud in school. He wondered if he was having a heart attack like Mr. Winkle in choir practice.

Josh unlatched the door to the storage room. He dusted cobwebs off the rusty birdcage and carried it up the attic stairs. Moments after he crumbled an oatmeal cookie on the floor of the cage, a mouse crept out from behind the trunk. It perked up its pink ears and began to nibble at the crumbs. Josh snapped the cage door shut. "Don't worry, little mouse. I'll take good care of you," he whispered. "I know what it feels like to be trapped."

Sitting down on Simon's bed, Josh looked out the attic window. He saw his grandparents in the meadow. Grumps was pacing back and forth yelling words at Nana. She sat silently, her arms crossed over her large chest. Josh felt a seeping sense of loneliness and confusion. He put his head down on the pillow and watched the mouse running around and around and around the cage. At least he had one friend on the island. At least he had Homer.

7.

Sun streamed through the attic window. Josh looked at his watch. It was 5:30 in the morning. Simon was snoring but Homer was awake, scampering around the birdcage. Josh checked to see that the door to his grandparents' bedroom was still shut. Then he tiptoed barefoot down the attic stairs. In the kitchen, he spread peanut butter and home-made blueberry jam on soggy saltines.

Sitting outside on the back porch, Josh felt the warm rays of dawning sun. He watched the birds swoop over the meadow. The hushed, motionless air smelled as fresh as his dad's pine shower soap. Josh wished his dad was sitting beside him. He'd talk to his dad about ways to get Grumps to like him. At home everyone liked him, even Buck, the meanest bully in school. Josh took a deep breath and counted to ten. Then he crumbled a cracker and tiptoed back up the attic stairs to feed Homer breakfast.

"How come you captured that dumb mouse?" Simon yawned.

"It's not dumb. It's cute. It's mine."

"Who else would want it?"

"Its name is Homer."

"Homer like that Greek dude?"

"No, Homer like in homerun, like in home, like where I wish we were right now."

"You can say that again," Simon groaned. He rolled over and pulled the sheet over his head. "The sun is blinding me."

Josh hopped off his bed. "I'll make a shade," he said. In the trunk Josh found folded sheets and a wool blanket covered in mothballs. Tying a string between two nails, he hung a yellowed bed sheet over the string to block out the sunshine.

"Ta-daah!" Josh cried.

"Thanks, Bro," Simon muttered. Sneezing three times, he climbed out of bed and opened the top bureau drawer. "Oh, gross!" Simon jumped back. "Mouse droppings! Mouse droppings are on my clean underpants!"

Josh grinned. He pulled blue jeans and a wrinkled Yankee T-shirt from his bulging suitcase and got dressed.

At breakfast Nana put two bowls of oatmeal on the table.

"I've got an idea," Simon whispered to Josh. Carrying a jar from the kitchen, he stirred a spoonful of peanut butter into the hot cereal. "Not bad," he said, smacking his lips.

"Way to go, Bro!" Josh whispered as he stirred a glob of peanut butter into his oatmeal.

Gramps walked into the dining room. Over his shoulder, he carried an ax, two hedge clippers, and a rusted saw. With his mean expression and bloodshot, bulging eyes, he reminded Josh of the evil killer in the movie, *Nightmare on Elm Street—Part 4.*

"Before we patch the roof," Gramps announced, "we'll clear the path to the cliff. The dwarf mistletoe is killing our trees. We must have had close to thirty blowdowns over the winter."

Nana took out her painting canvas and tied a straw hat under her sagging chin. "You'd better wear this," she said, holding out a bottle of sunscreen.

"But I *want* a tan," Josh protested.

"Mind what your grandmother says!" Gramps muttered. "She's a wise woman." He watched as Josh and Simon put dabs of sunscreen on their pale noses. "We'll be back by noon, Rosie," he said. He kissed his wife gently on the forehead and headed out the back door.

The path to the north end of the island was overgrown with vines, branches, and prickle bushes. Josh was glad he'd worn long pants. He and Simon trimmed with the clippers while Gramps sawed off the taller tree branches. Even though it was cool in the pine woods, perspiration dripped down the back of Josh's neck.

"I feel a tick!" Simon rolled up his shirt sleeve and squashed a tiny bug.

"No ticks on Seal Island," Gramps said, hacking at a branch. "No poison ivy, either." He put down the saw and leaned on the ax handle. Sweat was rolling off his whiskers. "The cave is farther down the trail," he panted.

"Cool!" cried Josh. He dropped the clippers and ran ahead on the overgrown path. He was tired of cutting branches. Already he had bleeding scratches and a blister on the palm of his hand. Simon ducked behind a tree and pulled out a book. Josh felt his big toe throbbing but he kept on running. He heard the sound of surf breaking on gigantic granite rocks jutting from the

47

sea. Right before the path ended on a cliff, Josh spotted two boulders leaning together. He peered into the narrow opening. "I found the cave!" he yelled.

Gramps walked stiffly down the path carrying the clippers and the ax. He pointed his hairy finger toward the rocks. "Watch your head. It's best to crawl on your stomach. If I had more trust in my bum hip, I'd take you on a guided tour."

"Don't look at me," said Simon. "I'm not going in there. There could be snakes and poison spiders."

Josh scratched his head. "How big is this cave?"

"Large enough to hold five or six people. One summer, years ago, scientists came up from Boston. They discovered a new species of blood-sucking cave bat. Said they'd name the bat after me."

"No way. I'm not going," Simon announced, cracking his knuckles.

"Bats are octurnal. They'd be sound asleep."

"Nocturnal, you moron! Can't you say anything right?"

Josh got down on his hands and knees. If he crawled through the cave, his grandfather would see that big-brain, know-it-all Simon was actually a sissy and a wimp. He wiggled his thin body into a dark hole about as wide as his gym locker in school.

When his eyes adjusted to the darkness, Josh saw ashes from a small fire and the words "Sam was here" written on the wall. It felt cool and damp and soggy inside the cave. Josh wanted to let out a loud Dracula laugh to listen to the echo, but he was afraid of waking up the bats. His Dad was famous for his Dracula laugh, especially on spooky nights when they went camping near the cemetery.

As Josh squeezed his body between the boulders at the other end of the cave, his foot dislodged a rock. Millions of slug bugs and crawly creatures wiggled from the sudden light into the safety of darkness. Josh stood up and brushed bugs and mud off his jeans. The front of his Yankee T-shirt was ripped and filthy.

"Cowabunga!" Josh cried as he slid down a huge, moss-covered boulder toward Gramps and Simon. "I saw a humungous spider!"

"No such word as humungous," Gramps said, patting him on the back. He brushed spider webs and sticks out of Josh's hair. "Rosie won't like the sight of that shirt," he chuckled.

"You look gross," Simon added.

On the way back to the house, Gramps handed Josh the saw and heavy work gloves. Josh sensed he'd risen in his grandfather's estimation. "Climb that spruce and cut down the dead branch hanging over the trail."

Gramps patted Josh on the back. "Can't wait to get you up on the roof, my boy. You're just like your mother. You climb like a spider monkey."

Simon went on ahead, reading his book as he walked. By the time they got back to the house, the sun was high in the sky. Josh could tell without looking at his watch that it was time for lunch.

"What happened to you?" Nana gasped.

"I crawled through the cave," Josh announced proudly.

"What a perfect time for a tidal pool bath!" Nana grabbed her straw hat and led Josh down the path to the beach. The high tide had filled a little rock basin. "The water in your bathtub has been warming all morning," she said cheerfully.

"I can't sit in that," Josh groaned. "It's covered with those sharp, white, barnacle things. Besides, the water is FREEZING!"

Josh washed his neck, bloody arms, and swollen toe in the tidal pool. The salt water stung his cuts and made his skin feel prickly. He longed for a real bath with foaming soap and a fluffy clean towel. He'd give up his allowance for a week just to sit in hot water.

After changing into a wrinkled Knicks T-shirt, Josh joined the others for a picnic lunch on the back porch. He noticed mouse teeth marks on the rim of the wooden salad bowl. He picked cucumbers and weird mushrooms out of his salad and took a bite of his tuna sandwich. "That was a wicked, cool cave," he said with his mouth full.

"Cool, but not wicked," Grandfather corrected. "I see that our grandson is quite adventurous."

"Crazy, you mean," said Simon.

Nana looked worried. "You are being careful, aren't you, dearie? I promised your parents I'd take excellent care of you both."

"Sure I'm being careful." Josh scratched a mosquito bite.

Gramps stroked his stubby, gray whiskers. "After my nap," he said, "we patch the roof."

Josh looked at the rickety, wooden ladder propped against the side of the workshop. Climbing around on a slippery, sloped roof seemed a lot more dangerous than climbing spruce trees. If Nana cared anything about her grandsons' safety, she'd tell old bug-eyes to patch the roof himself.

After lunch, Simon got his book and crawled into the hammock. Josh knew his brother wasn't really reading. He was staring at the weathervane on the chimney and thinking up excuses. He'd pretend to have a deathly fear of heights. He'd say that when he went to Mystic Seaport on a class trip, he got dizzy climbing just two feet up the boat's mast. Grumps would fall for his story. He'd let Simon read history books in the hammock. He'd force his other "adventurous" grandson to risk his life replacing rotten shingles. All Grumps wanted was slave labor, with no thanks attached.

The first trip ashore, Josh knew he'd have to escape. He already had a plan.

8.

Josh plotted his escape from Seal Island, Maine. Every day for a week his grandfather had barked out orders. In the broiling sun, Josh had scraped peeling red paint off the front door and repainted it Nana's favorite color, sky blue. His back ached from replacing rotten shingles on the leaking roof. He had cuts and bulging blisters on his hands from clearing trails. His nose stung from peeling sunburn.

All week Simon had been useless. He kept a book tucked under his belt. When Gramps wasn't looking, he'd creep behind a tree and read. Josh never stopped working. His bones felt like he'd caught arthritis and his skin itched from saltwater sponge baths in the tidal pool. Homesickness nibbled like a mouse at his aching heart.

The first trip ashore, Josh planned to make his move. He'd find a pay phone and make a collect call to his best friend, Zipper. He'd tell Zipper's mom about being forced into slave labor, and she'd wire money to the post office. He'd seen an ad on TV. You could wire money in less than one hour. With the cash, he'd buy a ticket and catch the bus back to New Jersey. He'd live with Zipper's family until his parents got back from England. Zipper's mom had always treated him like a second son.

Every night after dinner, Nana read *Treasure Island* by candlelight. Josh lay on his back and watched the dancing fire shadows on the ceiling as she read. This was the one moment in the day he looked forward to. When Nana read aloud, he could remember every detail, not like in school when he'd forget the main character's name. At the end of chapter five, Nana's voice was getting scratchy from talking in so many different accents. She closed the book and began to blow out the ring of candles that surrounded her armchair.

"Not so fast," Gramps said, re-lighting the candles and putting on his glasses. "Tomorrow we go ashore." He blinked his bulging, red eyes as he examined the tide calendar. "The *Odyssey* leaves for the mainland at nine a.m. sharp. The first stop is the post office. Then we'll buy groceries and get a new propane tank. Simon, my boy, when we get back to the island, I'll teach you how to hook up the refrigerator, stove, and water pump to the propane gas line."

Hot wax burned Josh's fingers as he carried the candle up the creaking attic stairs. He sat on his unmade bed and printed the address of his parent's hotel in London on a postcard of a lobster boat. Last summer he'd sent lots of postcards to his mom and dad from Boy Scout Camp. He'd written about hitting homers, playing miniature golf, getting to the advanced level of the ropes climbing course, catching a trout, and the night the kid from New York mushed a toasted marshmallow in his hair. On the island, there was nothing to report, only lists of forced work projects. He hadn't even had time to read one chapter in his summer reading book.

Simon wrote a note to his mom and dad and a three-page letter to Jen, his girlfriend. Josh saw no point in writing his best friend. He'd be back in New Jersey before Zipper could get the postcard. Soon the nagging homesick ache would go away. Soon he'd be back in his hometown where he belonged.

The next morning, Josh woke up before dawn. He was too nervous to sleep. He tossed on the sagging mattress and waited for the birds to start chirping. Even Homer lay silently in his cage. He was snuggled under a pair of Josh's dirty socks. When the sun came up, Josh stuck his toothbrush and all his spending money in his jeans pocket. He put on his good luck Phish T-shirt and raked his fingers through his mussed-up hair. Hanging the bed sheet over the window to block the sun, Josh tiptoed down the attic stairs.

Gramps sat silently at the head of the dining room table, waiting for his oatmeal.

"Good morning, Grandfather," Josh said. "You're up early."

"Always am, young man," Gramps replied. "Planning on brushing your teeth ashore, I see."

"I'm going to shower and freshen up at the winter house." Josh nervously fingered the money in his pocket. "How come you don't live ashore all year round, Gramps? I bet Nana would be happier living in Moxie Cove than she is living out here on an island."

"I ought to know what makes your grandmother happy," Gramps huffed. "I've lived with the woman for forty-seven years."

Josh thrust both fists into his baggy jeans pockets, "So what time are we leaving?" he asked.

"The boat departs at nine o'clock sharp. With so much weight on the return trip, I want to get back to the dock before low tide."

"Will the waves be big?"

"The harbor is as smooth as a seal's belly." Gramps tapped the barometer. "For the Muscongus Bay region today, I predict clear skies with light northwesterly winds."

"I almost got seasick on the last trip," Josh said as he spread peanut butter and raspberry jam on a line of saltine crackers.

"We'll toughen you up, my boy! You're a good worker. You've got more stamina than your brother, that's for sure."

Josh looked at his blistered hands and mosquito-bitten legs. He felt tough enough already. All he wanted was to rest up in front of the television. It would take weeks for his aching body to recover. "I'm going over to the cliffs to take pictures of the seals," he said. "I'm making friends with one of the babies."

"Seals have pups, not babies."

Josh took his camera off the fireplace mantel. When he got back to New Jersey, he planned to enter a photo contest. If he won the prize money, he'd buy video games for himself and a battery-operated TV for his grand-

mother. "I'll be back by 8:30," Josh called as the screen
door slammed behind him.

Josh jumped over fingers of light filtering through
the pines and pointed firs as he ran along the trail to
the cliffs. Stopping to pick tiny wild blueberries, he sat
on the ground and flipped berries into his mouth the
way he flipped popcorn at the movie theater. It wouldn't
be long now before he and Zipper could go to summer
blockbusters in air-conditioned theaters. Josh clicked
a picture of the cave to show Zipper and Kip and all his

friends at school. He scrambled over the high cliffs and down to the rocky shore.

Josh spotted about a dozen pitch-black seals sunning on a craggy ledge. He crept silently toward them. Hopping from rock to rock farther into the bay, he got up so close he could hear their snorts and low growling sounds. Balancing on a ledge dripping with wet seaweed, Josh held the camera to his eye and focused the zoom lens. Just as he snapped the picture, a wave broke over the rock. Josh lost his balance. In a rush of foaming backwater, he fell shoulder deep into the freezing sea.

"Help! I'm drowning!" Josh shrieked in a panicked voice. There was no one to hear his cry except the startled seals. Holding the camera above his head, he stumbled toward the shore. A wave broke on his back, pushing him under water with a sharp, frigid force. Josh swam a few yards and pulled himself onto a slippery, flat rock. On the crest of a rolling in-coming wave, he dove back into the water and body surfed to shore.

Josh stood up and staggered onto the rocky beach. His toes and fingers were numb. He sat trembling on a rock, draining salt water out of his sneakers. The soggy dollar bills in his pocket were safe but his camera and toothbrush had washed away.

Josh wrung the water out of his lucky Phish T-shirt. His peeling, sunburned arms were covered with goose bumps. Shivering, Josh decided to look for a short-cut back to the house. Instead of taking the winding path by the cave, he decided to cut straight across the center of the island. Already he could feel the symptoms of pneumonia setting in.

Josh pushed tall ferns and bush branches out of his way. He climbed under downed trees and scrambled over rocks covered with green moss and gray lichens. He rested for a moment and looked at a flower growing out of bare rock, its roots held invisibly in a tiny crack of soil. Glancing anxiously at his damp watch, he realized it had stopped ticking. Josh hurried on. When his wet sneakers sank into muddy marsh grass, he realized he'd wandered into a watery bog.

Totally disoriented, Josh stopped and looked in all directions. There were no familiar landmarks or rocks piled on the trail to mark which way to turn. Looking up, he saw a towering, dead tree with an enormous nest perched on top. A bird with a giant wing span circled above him in the air. It looked like a vulture waiting to pick his bones. A shiver of fear crackled through his body.

As Josh trudged through the soggy bog of tangled grasses, his right foot hit something hard. He bent over and picked up bones from a skull. Josh wondered if it was a dead animal or human remains. His feet felt locked in ooze. Maybe he was walking through quicksand!

Josh stood still, listening. If he could hear the waves, he could find the shore. If he found the shore, he could walk around the island until he came to the house. Perspiration dripped down his neck. Octopus arms of panic squeezed until he panted for breath. The only other time he'd felt so terrified was when he'd gotten lost and biked through a violent thunderstorm in New Jersey.

Able to hear only the wind and his heart pounding in his ears, Josh climbed a pine tree. From the top branches, he could see the ocean. Josh walked to the left of the sun, through the bog, toward the shore. By the time he had walked halfway around the island, the sun was directly above his head. As Josh rounded the point, he saw the dock and the house. There was no boat in the harbor. The *Odyssey* had left for Moxie Cove without him.

9.

Josh collapsed in exhaustion. He didn't care what Grumps had said about throwing rocks off the dock. In frustration, he hurled fistfuls of stones into the water. How dare they go ashore without him! Now he'd have to wait another whole week to escape from Seal Island. Josh cupped his two hands over his eyes and scanned the horizon. A lobster boat was pulling traps just outside the harbor. He could row out and plead for help, except that his body ached all over and he didn't know how to row.

Josh kicked more stones off the dock. If only he'd taken the cave path home. How come he always got lost? Simon NEVER got lost. He didn't mix up north and south and right and left. When the Boy Scouts went on a ten mile hike, they gave Simon the map and made him the navigator. Simon could remember strings of directions and whiz through books a thousand pages long.

Josh yanked off his wet sneakers. He wished Simon was the one born with dyslexia. That way Gramps would discuss Latin and boats and gas tanks with him instead of his brother. That way his grandfather might actually get to know him.

"There you are!" Nana cried, hurrying down the path holding her straw hat. "I was so worried about you."

Josh looked up, surprised. "How come you didn't go ashore?"

"I'd never leave a child alone on the island. Don't tell Hobs, but I washed my hair." She shook her wispy, white, waist-length hair in the wind. "Where have you been? You're drenched!"

"My new camera got swept away by a giant wave and my watch stopped and I almost drownded and now I'm getting sick."

Nana gasped. "Lord almighty! Let's get you into dry clothes."

"I got lost in some dumb swamp. That's why I missed the trip ashore. I really, really wanted to get to the mainland." Josh shivered. "Now my chest hurts, like I'm getting a heart attack."

Nana hugged him, even though his shirt was wet. Josh felt her big, soft breasts against his skin. She smelled of baby powder and shampoo. "Hobson dug up a few clams at low tide," Nana said taking his hand and walking toward the house. "I've made an odd chowder with herbs and powdered milk. Run up and take a hot shower. I won't breathe a word to your grandfather."

The thought of a hot shower took away the pain in his chest. Josh put his sneakers in the sun to dry and raced up the attic stairs to get a towel. After soaping his body in a weak flow of tepid water, he dried himself off and parted his hair for the first time in a week. The mirror was so cracked and foggy he barely noticed any pimples. Except for his peeling nose, his face looked good with a tan.

The smell of baking bread filled the kitchen. Josh felt a pang of intense hunger. Nana handed him a glass of fizzy medicine. "This will cure what ails you." She squinted at a tattered cookbook. "I'm baking Hob's favorite raspberry-rhubarb pie for dinner."

"How come you married Gramps?" Josh picked up a dishtowel and began to dry the mixing bowls. "I don't mean to be rude, but I've never met such a grouch in my life."

A slow smile spread over his grandmother's wrinkled face. "Hobson and I fell in love my second year in college. I was "from away," as they say in Maine. I grew up in Michigan but I applied to the University of Maine because of the drama department. I took a Latin course, don't ask me why. I was majoring in theater, you know. I was told I had a good deal of talent. I dreamed of performing Shakespeare in London or becoming a movie star in Hollywood. Instead, I was swept off my feet by a Latin professor! Hobson was so handsome and romantic back then. We eloped the week after I graduated."

"But I thought you were an artist," Josh said.

Nana shook her head. "I only took up painting after the tragedy."

"What tragedy?"

"When we lost our little Jacob. I thought your grandfather would lose his mind with grief when Jacob died. He kept on teaching, mind you, but all that wonderful wit and tenderness that I'd fallen in love with just dried up inside him. To be honest, I thought about packing up the girls and moving back to Michigan." Nana paused. "That's when I took up painting."

"How did Jacob die? Mom never told me she had a brother."

66

"It was on a Sunday morning. I went to church early to arrange the flowers on the altar. Hobson put Jacob down for his morning nap. When I got home from church, I went to check on the baby. He was lying on his stomach in his crib, only his little face had turned blue. He'd stopped breathing. Sudden Infant Death Syndrome they call it. To this day, I don't really understand what happened. I cried for months but your grandfather never shed a tear. Somehow he felt that Jacob's death had been his fault. He shelled himself up like a turtle. That's the way Hobs dealt with the grief."

"He's still shelled up, if you ask me," Josh said, then stood in silence as his grandmother spilled out more words.

"After Jacob's death, Hobs threw himself into his work. Everyone said he was a brilliant teacher. The students adored him. He's written several textbooks, you know. Hobs is not a bad man—not at all! When the University decided to cut the Latin Department and expand the Spanish Department, it forced Hobs into early retirement. That's what broke his spirit, not being able to teach. I thought you and Simon might cheer the old man up. That's one reason I asked your mother to send you boys to the island."

Josh swallowed hard. "This was YOUR idea?"

Nana nodded. "It helps your parents out, too, of course. They deserve a trip together, after all these years."

Josh dropped the dishtowel and ran to the back door. Out in the meadow, he sat on the ground and rocked back and forth, hugging his knees with his arms. Now he understood why his mother had insisted that they stay on the island. Josh took ten deep breaths and counted to 20 with each one. When he felt back in control, he opened the screen door. "Sorry Nana," he said. "I suddenly thought I was going to barf. I needed fresh air."

"The medicine will take effect any minute," Nana said reassuringly.

Josh stared out the dining room window. "So when will Gramps and Simon get back from Moxie Cove?" he asked.

Nana set two blue bowls of steaming clam chowder on the table. "First they'll do the laundry," she said sitting down, "then food shop and get the propane tank and have the mower blades sharpened at the hardware store. I doubt Hobs takes the time to weed my garden, though Lord knows it needs it. Hobs always stops off at the post office to pick up the mail. Hopefully, he'll remember to buy me the local newspaper. I never have a clue all summer long what's going on in town unless he remembers to buy me the paper."

"So what time will they get back?" Josh repeated.

"Before low tide, that's for sure. Your grandfather hates using the drain tide dock. It needs repairs in the worst way."

Josh pulled off a large hunk of warm bread. "Will you teach me to row, Nana? After your nap can we go out in the dory?"

Nana nodded. "I'll teach you to row and I'll teach you to play cards. The girls and I loved to play cribbage and gin rummy."

"Whenever we play cards, Simon always wins. I just want to learn how to row."

After stacking the dishes in the drying rack, Josh stuffed two peanut butter cookies in his pocket. The attic was hot and airless. It smelled of mothballs, fresh bread, and mildew. He opened the window and looked through the screen toward the mainland. The sound of country-western music from a lobster boat's radio drifted across the harbor. There was no sign of the *Odyssey*. Josh sprinkled cookie crumbs on top of Homer's head and opened his summer reading book.

Each time he turned a page, he pictured Jacob turning blue in the rusty, iron crib. Josh turned down the corner of page 8 and drifted into sleep.

"Ready to row?" Nana called up the attic stairs.

Josh awoke with a start. "I'll meet you on the dock in five minutes," he cried. Josh refilled Homer's water shell with rain from the leak bucket by his bed. Then he grabbed his soggy sneakers by the front door and ran down the path. Nana stood on the dock in her straw hat holding two red lifejackets.

"Think we're going to capsize?" Josh asked.

Nana shook her head. "Boaters should always wear a lifejacket, just as a general rule. One false move and Maine water temperatures can bring on hypothermia in no time. Always step on the centerline of a rowboat," Nana said, as she sat down on the stern seat.

Josh waited for the boat to stop rocking before he hopped onto the center of the middle seat. He sat down facing the front of the boat.

"You're facing the wrong way!" Nana chuckled. "Don't look toward the bow. Face me."

"But then I can't see where I'm going!"

"Look over your shoulder."

Josh turned around in his seat. He put the oars in the oarlocks and pulled with all his might. The right oar immediately popped out of the oarlock.

"Caught a crab!" Nana cried.

"Where?"

"Just an expression. That's what people say when an oar gets caught in the water. Don't slice the oars so deeply, and don't pull with such great force."

Josh repeated his grandmother's instructions under his breath. In the wind and current, it was hard to pull on both oars with equal strength. First the boat went in circles to the right. Then, after gaining more momentum, Josh smashed into a lobster buoy to his left. Nana stayed calm the whole time, even when the left oar dropped overboard and began drifting out to sea.

Josh was concentrating so hard on rowing, he didn't hear the *Odyssey* chugging back into the harbor. Not until he heard someone calling his name, did he look up. Standing in the middle of the lobster boat, he saw Simon. He was triumphantly waving a box of Sugar Frosted Corn Crunchies.

10.

Simon portioned out his half of the box of Sugar Frosted Corn Crunchies so carefully that it lasted for the next five days. Josh ate the last sweet bite of his cereal the day the box arrived. Except for the food shopping, Simon said going ashore with Gramps was torture, worse than getting his braces tightened. First he had to do three loads of laundry. Then he had to weed Nana's gardens in the broiling sun. He didn't even get to take a shower or watch one minute of television.

The days on Seal Island took on a predictable routine. Before breakfast, Josh crossed off another day in red ink on his Yankee Baseball calendar. While Simon nibbled sugar cereal and Josh ate oatmeal, Grumps would list the chores for the day. After lunch everyone had free time for one hour. Simon read in the hammock or worked on his battleship model. Josh practiced rowing up and down the harbor or walked over to the cliffs to eat wild raspberries and watch the sunning seals. By nightfall, when Nana lit the candles to read *Treasure Island,* Josh could hardly keep his eyes open.

Every morning Simon ate breakfast with a book in his face. Josh wanted to talk. "I saw a vulture's nest in the swamp," he said, trying to get his brother's attention.

"Vultures don't nest in swamps, you dope."

"Seriously, I saw this humungous nest on top of a dead tree. I spotted it the day you went ashore without me."

Simon dropped his book. "Let's go check it out!"

"Not so fast." Gramps scratched his scruffy whiskers. He stood up stiffly and tapped the barometer. "With the full moon, we'll have what we call a drain tide, at least two feet lower than normal. It's the perfect time to rebuild the dock. I'll row you boys over to Gull's Point to collect rocks. Get your lifejackets and meet me on the dock in five minutes."

"Okey-dokey!" Simon muttered.

As Josh jumped onto the middle seat of the dory, he asked, "Can I row? Yesterday, Nana taught me how to feather the oars."

Gramps slipped the heavy wooden oars into the oarlocks. "I'll row," he said gruffly, pulling the boat away from the dock.

Josh trailed his fingers in the icy water. "I see a jellyfish!" he cried.

Simon looked up from his book. "Do you notice any scales, fins, or gills?" he asked smugly.

"No, but look! It's floating near that batch of sea grass."

"Then it's not a fish! Ha ha!" Simon gloated. "Got you again! It can't be a fish unless it has scales, fins, or gills. It says so right here in my book."

Josh wished he had the butterfly net. He'd catch the slimy glob of non-fish and plop it on top of his brother's big, fat head!

Gramps pulled hard on the oars. "Stop quibbling. When we get to the point, fill the buckets with as many flat rocks as you can carry." He looked over his shoulder and pulled harder on the left oar, steering the boat toward the shore. "A southerly wind is picking up."

When the dory ran aground on Gull's Point, Josh took off his sneakers and rolled up his long pants. He jumped over the side of the rowboat and sank up to his ankles in mud. "This feels cool," he cried, watching the mud ooze through his toes. Little water spouts from buried clams spurted around his ankles.

"Yuck!" cried Simon. "I'm not walking in that glop."

"Get out and help your brother," Grandfather ordered.

"Okey-dokey!" Simon made a face like he'd been stung by a wasp. He jumped over the side of the dory and tiptoed through the mud, holding up his pant legs. The gulls cackled loudly as Simon filled the rusty bucket with flat stones. He made Josh carry the rocks over the mud flats to the boat. Josh dumped buckets of stones into the middle of the dory, under Gramp's feet.

"Hop back aboard. Any more weight and we'll sink!" Gramps handed Josh the left oar. "Sit here and do what I say," he instructed.

Josh squeezed onto the seat next to his grandfather. He gripped the oar with both hands. Wanting to impress his grandfather, he gave a powerful tug. Instead of dipping the oar into the water, it skimmed over the surface of a wave and bounced out of the oarlock. Josh lurched off the seat and landed on the heap of rocks.

"You okay, Bro?"

Josh nodded, rubbing his bottom. "I'm not used to so much weight."

"Rowing is not as easy as it looks, my boy. Sit here between my legs and put your hands on top of mine."

Josh felt his grandfather's chest heaving hard behind him. He put his fingers over his grandfather's enormous hairy hands and pulled with a steady, graceful rhythm. The oars dipped in and out of the water as the boat glided back toward the drain tide dock.

"You're getting the hang of it now, Joshua, just like your mother. Once your mother rowed all the way to the mainland. She was a real pro when it came to rowing." Gramps lifted the right oar and pulled the boat alongside the drain tide dock. "Put on your shoes. I've sewed up too many cut feet in my day."

The thought of Grumps jabbing a needle and thread through a gash on the bottom of his foot made Josh quickly force his muddy toes into his sneakers. He climbed over the side of the boat and jumped onto the drain tide dock. Crabs scurried over the seaweed and hid under pieces of slippery brown kelp. Working to keep his balance, Josh arranged the rocks in neat rows. By the time the dory was empty, the drain tide dock was three inches higher.

"That's enough lifting for one day," Gramps said. "You boys deserve a little excitement. With the tide this low, we might get the boat into the water caves. Some say the Robbing Rekowski Brothers stashed their spoils right here on Seal Island."

"Cool!" Josh cried. "Maybe we'll find treasure!" Looking at the ocean swells, Josh climbed into the bow of the boat. "You can row, Gramps," he said.

Simon clung to the seat in the stern as the dory hit the pitch and roll of the waves outside the protected harbor. By the time the boat rounded the north end of the island, a southerly breeze had cooled the air. Billows of fog rolled in from the sea like blankets of gray cotton candy. Gramps pointed to the cliffs jutting from the sea. "Between those boulders," he said, "there's a water cave."

Josh looked through the thickening fog at the shore line. He saw ocean surf breaking with foaming white spray into the mouth of the cave. "You mean you want to row in THERE?" he asked, his eyes growing wider.

"Where is your sense of adventure? Who knows what lies on that watery ledge. Some say gold; some say drugs. Don't you boys want to find the loot?"

"No thank you," Simon said in a shaky voice. "I don't think Nana would approve of this. It's not safe. One big wave and the dory will be smashed to smithereens on those rocks."

"He's right, Gramps. We could easily get drownded," Josh agreed.

Simon chewed nervously on his lower lip. "This fog is unreal. I can hardly see Josh or the end of the oars. We'll NEVER find our way back to the dock!"

"Stop whining and sit still," Gramps ordered. His voice sounded urgent. "Joshua, keep a lookout for submerged rocks. As long as we can hear waves breaking on the shoreline, we know we're near the island, not heading out to sea." Every few strokes, Gramps stopped rowing to listen. The only sounds were the lapping of the waves against the side of the boat and the crash of breaking waves on the shore.

After what seemed like an hour of rowing, Josh said, "Maybe we should be going in the ostipit direction."

"Opposite, not ostipit," came a shaky voice from the stern.

"Hear that squawking?" Gramps lifted the dripping oars. "We must be passing Gull's Point." He continued rowing, grunting with each powerful stroke. Beads of sweat dripped off his whiskers. Josh could see the headlines now: "Dead Bodies of Three Men Found after Days Adrift at Sea." Suddenly he felt smothered in a cold cocoon of fear. He could hardly breathe. Josh took a string of shallow breaths. Two feet ahead, he saw the jagged silhouette of a rock just below the surface. "Gramps! Row to the right!" he yelled. "I mean to the left!"

Gramps yanked on the left oar, then the right. As the boat scraped over the submerged shoal, there was a sickening grinding sound. A gushing spout of water suddenly spurted up in the stern, under Simon's seat.

"Bail with the bucket." Gramps barked.

"But the bucket leaks!" Simon cried.

"Do as I say!" Gramps kept rowing, hard. Every few seconds, he held up the oars, listening for the sound of the waves breaking on the shore.

"What's that sound?" Simon whispered. He waited to throw another bucket of seawater over the side of the boat. "I heard a clanking noise."

"I know that sound!" Josh cried excitedly. "It's that metal hook thing banging against the flagpole!"

Simon jumped up, causing the boat to tip wildly. "Way to go, Gramps! I don't believe it! We made it back to the dock!"

Gramps's sunken cheeks filled into a smile. "Good job, men! We'll ground the dory on the beach before she sinks." His voice had a distinct tone of relief. "Keep bailing!"

Josh and Simon pulled the dory over the mud flats to the beach, above the high tide line. They jogged barefoot up the path to the house. Suddenly, Nana emerged like a ghost from the fog. She ran past them. "Where's Hobson?" she cried in a panic.

Before they could say a word, Nana threw her arms around her husband's neck. Her body shook with sobs.

"Sorry we're late for lunch, Rosie," is all he said.

Josh waited for his grandmother on the path. "Did you think we got drownded?" he asked. Nana nodded, choking back a sob.

Josh wrapped both arms around his grandmother and hugged her long and dearly.

11.

Rowing to the water cave without finding hidden treasures had made Gramps stiff and meaner than a hornet. He told Rosie he'd have climbed into the cave himself, if it weren't for his bum hip. Josh felt secretly pleased to see his grandfather in pain. As long as he had to lean on his walking stick, he wouldn't attempt another hair-brained treasure expedition.

It took three days for the patch on the bottom of the dory to dry. After lunch, instead of rowing up and down the harbor, Josh wandered into the workshop. He'd quit building the model of the aircraft carrier. Instead, he'd started collecting pebbles, shells, beach glass, feathers, bark, and dried grasses to build a deluxe castle habitat for Homer. Josh glued snail shells on the turrets and found a round rock the size of his fist for the banquet table. He made a moat out of curled birch tree bark. With Simon's dental floss, he rigged up a moving drawbridge made out of a rotten shingle from the roof.

One afternoon, after his nap, Gramps hobbled into the workshop. "Thought you could use this," he said, handing Josh a dried crab shell.

"Cool! The two claws can hold the flag over the drawbridge."

Gramps's thin lips stretched into a grin. "Time to cut the grass," he announced, limping out of the shop.

Josh took momentary pity on his grandfather. "Need help with the mawnlower?" he asked.

"The word is lawnmower, you stupid idiot!" Simon called from the hammock.

Josh swallowed a hot bubble of anger. Every time Simon called him stupid, it made his blood boil. Josh picked up the bucket where he kept his pet crabs. Slipping his hands into Nana's gardening gloves, he fumbled through the wet seaweed until he found Orton and Gillingham, the two biggest crabs. Their pincer claws reached out wildly in self-defense. Josh tiptoed over to the hammock. He dangled Orton over Simon's head. "Stop calling me stupid idiot, you wordy-nerdy wimp!"

Simon sprung out of the hammock. The book fell upside down on the ground. "You made me lose my place!" he shouted. "Get those creature away from me!"

"Keep calling me stupid and they'll be in your bed!"

Simon made a fist, grabbed his book, and climbed back into the hammock. "You wouldn't dare!" he snarled, searching for his place.

"Try me!" Josh grinned as he pushed the squeaky lawnmower down the grass path toward the blueberry patch. Nana was bending over a bush, dropping blueberries into an old coffee can.

"Want to see a huge bird's nest?" he asked.

Nana straightened her back. "You know how Hobson is about keeping to his routine. He'll want his cup of hot tea and a cookie at 4 o'clock."

"We'll be back long before then," Josh said. Leaving the lawnmower in the middle of the path, he pulled his grandmother toward the cliff path. "It's not a vulture's nest. Simon says it's a genuine eagle's nest! He looked it up in his *Maine Coast Bird Book*."

Nana followed Josh along the forest path. "Speaking of nests," she said, stopping suddenly, "look at this one. You can tell it's an eider's nest by the down feathers stuck to those cracked eggs. The female plucks the down out of her breast and covers the eggs. That keeps the eggs warm and protects them from predators."

"Cool!" Josh knelt down and examined the abandoned nest.

The smell of bayberry and juniper gave the air a fresh, sweet aroma. As they walked over a carpet of green moss and pine needles, Nana picked a bouquet of wood lilies and wild daisies. "If you take that path," she said, pointing to an overgrown trail, "you'll come across a tiny graveyard."

"No way!" Josh cried excitedly. "Show me."

Nana pushed ferns and prickly raspberry bushes out of her path as she approached a small plot of weathered headstones. "In the old days, there were several houses on Seal Island. The people raised sheep, fished, and farmed as best they could. Some poor souls even spent the winter out here. I just don't know how they managed. Look at this grave." Nana pointed to a small, tilting headstone. ABIGAIL . . . DIED AT FIVE DAYS OLD.

"I like this one better," Josh said, bending over to read another moss covered grave. "It says LEVERETT DAVIS . . . DIED AT THE AGE OF 106 IN THE YEAR OF OUR LORD 1852. Do you and Gramps want to be buried on the island?" Josh asked.

"Sprinkle my ashes over the blueberry patch. That may sound odd, but to my mind, it's the most splendid spot on God's good earth."

"What about Gramps?" Josh asked.

"Good question. Every time I bring up the subject of death, he discusses the weather. He won't even write a will. Even after his old friend Wink, from the University, died of pneumonia this past winter, he still refuses to talk about it."

Josh looked into his grandmother's sad, wise eyes. She talked to him like a real teenager, not just some little kid. If he went back to New Jersey, who would listen to her stories? Simon was too busy reading books and building models to pay attention. Gramps only spoke when he wanted something. For a man smart enough to teach Latin, he didn't seem to say much of interest to his wife.

"Last night the moon was round as a dime! I remember when Hobs used to take me and the girls out for moonlit harbor sails. That was years and years ago. Now he refuses to leave the house after dark, even to go to the movies."

"You could always rent a video," Josh suggested, leading his grandmother back to the trail. Hearing the distant sound of surf breaking on the cliffs, Josh headed off the path and into the grassy swamp. Nana quickly spotted the eagle's nest at the top of the dead pine tree.

"What a marvelous subject for a painting!" she exclaimed. "Let's get Simon's camera and take lots of pictures. If there isn't enough time to finish the painting by the end of the summer, I'll bring the photos to my studio in Moxie Cove. Hobs would just love a painting of our eagle's nest in the winter house. It will remind him so of the island. Perhaps I'll paint our old sailboat in the background, just to bring back memories."

As Nana poured afternoon tea, Gramps stood up from the table to watch a boat with a tall mast sail into the harbor. "That boat belongs to Dr. Phillips and his wife," he said, chewing prunes from the box. "They sail down east from Fenwick every summer."

Josh looked through the binoculars. "Simon! Come quick! Two girls on deck."

Simon dropped his book and grabbed the binoculars from Josh's hand. He ran his tongue over his upper lip.

"Josh is becoming an excellent rower," Nana said. "Perhaps you boys would like to take the dory and row out to welcome these nice people to our harbor.

Bitsy Phillips is such an interesting lady. She works in television. Their daughters must be about your age by now."

"Great idea!" Josh cried. "I'll get two lifejackets from the shop."

"Bring three," Gramps said, spitting out a prune pit.

"Okey-dokey," Simon mumbled under his breath.

Rowing toward the sloop, Josh flexed his arm muscles to impress his brother. Gramps watched his every move from the bow but Simon paid no attention. He was thumbing through *The Maine Coast Bird Book*. He had identified sandpipers, black-bellied plovers, ospreys, and a blue heron by the time Josh pulled the dory alongside the visiting sloop.

"Come aboard, Hobson!" A handsome man in a faded blue shirt and tomato-red pants bent down to help Gramps onto the boat. Josh wished he'd combed his hair. He grinned at the girls. One had short blonde hair and one had frizzy red hair with neon-green braces on her front teeth.

"I'd like you to meet my grandsons, Simon and Joshua. They're visiting Rosie and me for the month."

"Pleased to meet you," the doctor said with a vise-grip hand shake. "You remember Wendy and Deb and my wife, Bitsy." A smiling woman wearing a cap that said *CBS News* on the brim appeared on deck.

"We were just talking about you," she said. "My girls simply adore coming to Seal Island. It's always the highlight of our cruise."

"Mind if we anchor in your harbor for a night or two?" the doctor asked.

"By all means! We're going ashore tomorrow to shop but you're welcome to use the beach and walk the trails." Gramps's voice actually sounded friendly.

"Stay as long as you want," Josh added eagerly. "Me and Simon can take you to see the seals and the cave."

"Simon and I," his grandfather corrected.

"I'm crazy about spelunking!" said the girl with the frizzy hair.

"What a coincidence!" Simon tried to keep his voice from cracking. "Spelunking is a favorite hobby of mine as well."

"Me too," said Josh. Whatever it was, he hoped they could do it in the morning, before he left for New Jersey.

After a short visit, Josh bulged his tan arm muscles as he rowed the dory back to Seal Island. The girl with the frizzy, red hair gave a quick, shy wave. "See you tomorrow!" she called.

Tomorrow was Saturday. Tomorrow was the long-awaited trip ashore. Tomorrow was the day that Josh would have to make his move.

12.

Josh carried the basket of dirty laundry to the dock, as well as bags of trash for the Moxie Cove dump. He followed his grandmother down the dock ladder and into the lobster boat for the trip ashore.

Nana propped her swollen feet on a pile of empty canvas grocery bags. "What a great summer," she grinned. "Having you boys on the island is such a treat!" Tying a bandanna tightly over her ears, she gave Josh's knee a loving pat.

As Seal Island disappeared into the haze, Josh stared into the boat's foamy, white wake, lost in thought. After he'd caught the bus to New Jersey, he imagined Gramps calling the Moxie Cove police to report a missing person. He'd be stomping his work boots and ranting at Nana that he'd warned her this would happen. The po-

lice would e-mail his parents' hotel in England, demanding their return. His mom and dad would get emergency plane tickets and fly home, sick with worry. They'd accuse him of ruining the summer for the entire family.

At that moment, Josh made a painful decision. He decided to endure two more weeks of teasing and slave labor on Seal Island. That way no one could ever call him a quitter. Besides, he hadn't finished Homer's castle and he was becoming a darn good rower, a much better rower than Simon.

Josh pulled two crumpled postcards from his jeans pocket. He borrowed a pen from Simon. Simon always kept ballpoint pens clipped to his shirt pocket in case he needed to make notes or list birds, bugs, and flowers in his nature journal.

Deer Mom and Dab,

How are you? I am terrable. Me and Simon do chors for Grumps (thats what we call him) all day long. He makes us clime up danjerous laders and hammer shingles into the roof that leeks eggzackly over my bed. He forsus us to chop down bushes with thorns. I've got lots of bluddy cuts and blisters. I caught a pet mowse and six pet crabs but Grumps said I can't bring them home. Simon reads books all day. He's no fun. How is Englind? I miss you very, very, very much and I'm still sick.

Your loving son,
Josh

Deer Ziper,

Me and Simon are still up in Mane visiting my grandparnts. It is real cool here. We may find tresur in a cave. I'm making an awsome casle for my pet mowse. Two realy cute grils just saled in on a boat. I think the oldest one likes me. Ive seen 100s of seals. I may win a prise Ive taken so many seal picktures, more than 2 rolls. I use Simon's camra cause mine got washed away the day I almost drownded. How is baseball? Have you made any more homeruns? Say hi to Kip and Coach Ward. I lerned how to row.

Your freind,
Josh

When they got ashore, Josh put the cards in the mailbox at the end of the Moxie Cove boat dock. After a trip to the town dump, Gramps drove to the winter house, about a mile out of town. The house had a water view and cable TV. The clam shells on the driveway made a cracking sound under the tires of the rusty pick-up truck.

After Nana washed her hair, Josh took a blasting hot shower with foaming green soap. For the first time since the dribble shower on the island, he didn't itch from caked sunscreen, sweat, and the prickly salt residue from the tidal pool.

Nana handed Gramps the grocery list and went outside to weed the gardens. Josh and Simon jumped into the back of the pick-up truck. They had a grocery list of their own.

At the Shop 'N Save supermarket, Simon put two six-packs of Coke into a plastic carry basket. Josh hurried up and down the aisles until he found the breakfast cereals. He grabbed two jumbo boxes of Chocolate Sugar Puffs and met Simon in the candy aisle. They collected bags of jelly beans, gummy bears, and candy bars to put in the grocery basket. Gramps stood in the check-out line, hands on his hips, tapping his foot. As he inched ahead in the long line of tan summer people, he spotted Josh and Simon.

"Put that junk back!" he demanded.

"But Gramps, we have our own money. We'll pay for this stuff with our saved-up allowance," Simon said.

"Sugar gives you quick energy," Josh added.

"I said, put it back!" Gramps's voice boomed so loud that the girl behind the cash register stopped chewing her bubble gum and stared. "I've got enough trouble lugging all this food out to the island without adding extra weight."

Hot sparks of fury exploded in Josh's brain. "That's it! I'm out of here!" he cried. Dropping the grocery basket in the middle of the checkout line, he marched out of the store and across the street to the gas station. Feeding coins into the public pay phone, Josh punched "O" for operator. "I want to make a call to Mrs. Winson in Ledgewood, New Jersey," he said. His heart thumping, he listened to the phone ring and ring in Zipper's kitchen. "Dial it again!" he pleaded. "This is an emergency."

Simon ran across the street. "Hurry up, Josh!" he cried frantically. "Get in the truck! Gramps says he's going to leave town without you!"

Josh listened to the endless ringing. Not even the answering machine picked up. Maybe Zipper and his family had gone to the Jersey Shore. Maybe they'd be away for a whole week. Josh slowly replaced the receiver and felt in the slot for his quarters. He took shallow gulps of air and tried to count to ten.

Simon put his arm around his brother's shoulder. "Keep your cool, Bro. Gramps let me buy a bag of candy," he whispered, handing Josh a chocolate bar. "And I saw a box of Frosted Bran Flakes when I put the groceries in the truck."

"Thanks!" Josh unwrapped the candy bar and stuffed his mouth with chocolate. The sweet, thick taste gave him courage. Without another word, he followed his brother back to the Shop 'N Save.

Gramps sat in the truck, beeping the horn. Simon jumped into the front seat. "Sorry to keep you waiting, Gramps. Josh had to run over to the gas station to use the men's room." Simon handed Josh another chocolate bar.

Josh climbed into the truck. He sat silently next to his brother, refusing to speak. When the pick-up truck pulled into the crunching driveway, Nana waved from the vegetable garden. She had filled a straw basket with lettuce, zucchini, tomatoes, and zinnia flowers. The clean clothes and bed sheets were neatly folded in the wicker laundry basket by the driveway.

"I missed you boys!" she cried, giving Josh a quick hug. "How was the grocery store?"

"Just great," Josh mumbled.

"The tide will be high enough for the big dock if we leave after lunch. I thought you kids might like to grab a bite to eat at Hank's Clam Hut next to the dock. Your mother always loved the fried clams and chocolate milkshakes. She and Hank's twin boys went to high school together. He'd be thrilled to see our Susie's handsome sons!"

"Mom never drinks milkshakes any more," Josh said as he helped load the laundry basket and propane gas tank into the truck. "She's always trying to stay thin." He wondered if his mother would turn fat with flabby arms and chins like Nana when she got old. Even if she gained a hundred pounds, though, it was better to be fat and loving than bone-thin and mean like his grandfather.

Simon ran inside the house to part his hair in front of a real mirror. He flushed the toilet, even for a pee, before he left the bathroom. Looking very pleased with himself, he climbed into the back of the truck. Josh raked his fingers through his messed-up hair and turned his baseball cap around backward. Smelling Simon's lemon cologne reminded him that the two girls were waiting on Seal Island for their return.

13.

Josh felt a curious sense of relief as the lobster boat chugged into the harbor. Moxie Cove had been hot and mobbed with tourists. Cars and campers with out-of-state license plates clogged the narrow roads. Returning to Seal Island gave Josh an unexpected sense of pine-fresh peacefulness.

"The doctor and his family must be ashore," Gramps yelled over the sound of the motor. "Their dinghy is tied to our dock."

Josh ran his fingers through his wind-blown hair. He wished he'd brought a comb. Simon had a comb in the pocket with his pens, but he never let anyone use it, for fear of getting lice.

At the house, there was no sign of the doctor and his family. Gramps showed Simon how to hook the new propane gas tank to the refrigerator line. Josh wanted to help but he was still too angry to speak to his grandfather. He was putting away the groceries when a voice called, "Anyone home? Thought we'd stop by to say hello!"

Gramps quickly limped into the bedroom and shut the door. It was time for his afternoon nap. Nana ran to the front door, delighted to have company. "Join us for coffee?" she chirped. "Where are the girls?"

"Sunbathing on the cliffs," the doctor replied. "Deb crawled through the cave but Wendy chickened out!"

Simon dropped his book. "Josh and I are going out for a walk," he announced, taking the comb out of his shirt pocket.

On the forest path, Josh hopped over slivers of sunlight filtering through the tall tree branches. When they got to the cliffs, he spotted the girls taking photos of the sunning seals. "Tell me their names again," he said to Simon.

"The blonde is Wendy and the redhead is Deb."

"What's up?" Josh called as he approached the girls. "I call that little guy Flipper. He's my favorite seal."

The blonde shifted her weight from one tan leg to the other. "He's cute!" she said. "How long have you guys been on the island?"

"Two weeks," Josh replied. "What grade are you in?"

"I'm in tenth and Deb is going into eighth. What about you?"

"I'm going into eighth too," Simon said. "My brother should be going into seventh but he's got dyslexia. He stayed back in first."

"I don't believe it!" cried the girl with frizzy hair. "I've got dyslexia too! We found out when I was in second but I didn't stay back."

"I named my pet crabs Orton and Gillingham. That's an inside joke," Josh said, grinning at Deb.

"Unbelievable! Here we are on a remote island and we both got taught the exact same phonics program!"

Simon looked at Wendy and rolled his eyes. Suddenly dozens of gulls shrieked calls of alarm. "Oh man, look at that!" Simon cried.

"It's a vulture!" shrieked Wendy.

"That, folks, is a genuine baldheaded eagle!" Simon paused for effect. "That explains why the gulls are squawking. As predators, gulls and eagles are natural enemies."

Josh had only seen a bird that big in horror movies. It looked like a flying seesaw, its wingspan was so wide. "I know where that eagle built its nest. Want to see?"

"No way! That creature is big enough to attack a human."

"Don't worry," Josh said reassuringly. "Eagles never attack unless they're hungry. There's plenty to eat on Seal Island."

"How do you know so much about eagles?" Simon asked. "I'm the one reading the bird books. Bet you don't know the name of THAT bird." Simon pointed to a brown bird with a yellow head.

Josh shrugged his shoulders.

"Let's go find the eagle's nest," Deb said. "I've got my camera."

Josh led the girls and his brother off the cliff path toward the swamp. Every few steps, Simon stopped to identify a plant or a bug. Josh wondered whether his brother was making up Latin names just to impress the girls.

"You're like a walking encyclopedia!" Wendy said. "Deb and I go for intelligent men."

Simon grinned, "Well, you found *one!*"

Josh wanted to belt his brother. He took a gulp of air, counted to twenty under his breath, and kept on walking.

"Darn this hair!" Deb moaned. "I can't see where I'm going. Once, I tried to press it straight on the silk setting of Mom's iron but it just curled up again. It's like my Mom's hair. It's hopeless."

Wendy reached over and ruffled Simon's hair. "You look older than an eighth grader. You look more my age, like a kid in high school."

Simon flashed a confident smile. "I'm in the accelerated program. I take courses most kids can't get until ninth grade," he said, cracking his knuckles.

Josh jumped over a wet tangle of marsh grass. Simon was so busy bragging to the girls that he stepped directly into the muddy bog. "You made me ruin my white Nikes!" he groaned. "Where on earth are you taking us? Shouldn't we be walking to the southwest?"

"It won't be long now!" Josh tried to make his voice sound confident. When he'd taken Nana to see the nest, he'd found it right away. "It's in a really tall tree."

"Of course it's in a tall tree," Simon said sarcastically. "Everyone knows that eagles build high to protect their young. They aren't really bald, you know. People call them bald because of their white head feathers." Simon bent down to pull up his muddy sock. "Eagles are the symbol of power and courage," he continued. "They're becoming extinct because pesticides have weakened the eggs so they don't hatch. Eagles have razor sharp talons. They swoop down and grab snakes and mice. Actually, duck is their favorite food. They tear their prey into pieces. Owls always eat their prey whole. Owls have no sense of smell. They can even eat skunk."

"How do you know so much?" Wendy asked.

"I read," Simon replied simply.

"He's a nerd." Josh pointed to the top of a dead tree. "See, look at that!"

Deb pushed fizzing, red ringlets away from her eyes. She stared up at the nest. "Wow! It's HUGE!"

Suddenly, there was a rushing, flapping sound. The eagle circled above the nest. "Let's get out of here!" Wendy shrieked.

Simon stood frozen, staring at the bird. "That eagle must have over a seven-foot wingspan," he murmured in amazement.

"Quick! Get under cover!" Josh pulled at Simon's arm. They ran together behind the girls toward the protection of the forest.

Once they were safely hidden under the trees, Deb paused on the forest path, panting. "Look at this. The dew has transformed this spider web into a glistening necklace of pearls."

Josh knelt down beside her. "You talk like a poet," he said, poking the web with a stick.

"My cat poem got published in the *Fenwick Gazette*," Deb said, pushing hair out of her eyes.

"I'm into art, myself." Josh cleared his throat. "My grandmother is an artist." Josh picked up pieces of curling, white tree bark. "I can use more bark for the moat," he said. "I'm making a castle for my pet mouse. It's kind of like a giant sculpture."

"Can I see it?" Deb asked. She swirled strands of wild hair into a bun and pushed a thick twig through the tight knot.

Josh nodded. "Hopefully Grumps won't be working in the shop. I can't stand the man. He won't even let us buy stuff at the grocery store with our own money. All he does is boss me and Simon around. Sometimes I wish the old grouch would just drop dead."

"You shouldn't talk that way about your grandfather."

"He treats me like an idiot! I'm the one who does all the work but he only talks to Simon."

"I think you're cool," Deb said. "I'd talk to you any day."

The grin froze on Josh's lips. "Did you hear that?" he asked.

Deb listened. "It sounds like firecrackers."

"Sounds like gunfire to me. Does your dad hunt ducks or rabbits or something like that?" Before Deb could answer, there was another sudden string of popping sounds.

"Take cover!" Simon yelled from farther down the path. "Some crazy is shooting a gun!"

"Deb, stay back!" Josh raced along the forest path toward the cliffs. The popping sound seemed to be coming from the water. When he got to the boulders above the sea, Josh peeked out from behind a jagged rock. Just off shore, he saw a man in a lobster boat aiming a rifle at the seals.

"STOP! Get out of here, you murderer!" Josh ripped off his shirt and began waving it frantically in the air. The man looked up, took one last shot, and then revved the boat's motor.

"What? Are you nuts?" Simon panted. "You could have been shot!"

Deb scrambled onto the cliff. "Are you all right?" she cried.

Josh pulled the shirt back over his head. His fingers were trembling. "Did he hit any?" Flipper's earless head bobbed near the ledge. All the seals had wiggled off the rocks and plunged into the sea. The water around the rocks was turning an ugly red.

"We've got to call the Coast Guard!" Josh cried. "We can use Gramps's cell phone." Josh began to race along the forest trail toward the house. "Emergency!" he yelled at the top of his lungs. "Get the telephone!"

14.

Josh raced through the meadow toward the house, frightening a family of field mice on the path. The doctor jumped up from his lawn chair. Gramps stood up stiffly.

"What's wrong?" called the doctor. "Where are the girls?"

"There's been a shooting!" Josh cried. "Get the cell phone. Call the Coast Guard!"

The doctor's wife clutched her husband's arm. "Where are my babies?" she wailed.

"Your girls are fine," Josh panted as he hopped up the stone steps to the back porch. "It's the seals. A lobsterman tried to kill our seals!"

Deb and Wendy's mother fell back into the lawn chair. "Oh, thank God!" she sighed in relief.

Simon and Deb ran out of the forest onto the meadow path. "Wendy tripped," Deb yelled. "She's bleeding."

The doctor and his wife jumped back up and headed for the woods.

"But what about the seals?" Josh cried. "Doesn't anyone care about the murdered seals?"

Wendy limped out of the trees into the meadow. She was holding bloody fingers over her knee. Her father met her on the path. He knelt down to examine the cut. "Just a surface wound," he announced. "Nothing to worry about."

"My, my, so much excitement!" Nana exclaimed. Josh had never seen his grandmother look happier. "Won't you join us for dinner? I can cook up a huge pot of spaghetti."

Gramps slumped back in his chair. His bulging, bloodshot eyes had a glazed look. Josh could tell that his grandfather had had enough conversation for one day.

"That would be just delightful!" cried the girls' mother. "What a treat not to cook in that teeny ship's galley! We'll bandage Wendy's knee, change into warmer clothes, and be back in no time."

While Simon walked with Wendy and Deb to the dock, Josh paced back and forth on the back porch.

"Aren't you going to do something, Gramps? Aren't you going to call the Coast Guard? What we saw was a criminal offense!"

"These things happen, Joshua." Gramps stroked his prickly whiskers. "When we were ashore, I heard Bart telling the postman that seals were ripping his nets. If he can't catch herring for bait, then he can't lobster. If he can't lobster, his wife and five kids go hungry."

"But people don't have to SHOOT the seals! Seals have rights too, you know. At least we should report the man with the gun. I'll bet it's not even legal to carry a rifle on a lobster boat." Josh shivered. A blanket of chilly fog had swept over the island. He ran inside the house and returned wearing his Yankee sweatshirt and carrying the black box in his hand. "What's the Coast Guard's telephone number?" he demanded.

"This is not what I'd call an emergency," Gramps said abruptly. "That lobster boat is long gone."

"Tell me the number," Josh insisted. "If anyone tries a stunt like this again, I'll order a patrol boat out here to arrest them."

"In a bona fide emergency, punch 1-911-SOS-HELP. May I remind you once again, Joshua, that you are not to use this phone without my permission.

"I know! I know!" Josh grumbled. He carried the black box back inside the house, slamming the screen door behind him.

Josh was on his way up the attic stairs to comb his hair when Nana called from the kitchen, "Be a lamb, dearie, and come set the table."

Taking eight forks out of the silverware box, Josh watched his grandmother stir onions, garlic, and thin-sliced zucchini in the iron frying pan. She was singing opera and steaming the clams that Gramps had dug up at low tide. Josh wondered if Orton and Gillingham were in the pot.

"Such a helpful boy!" Nana cried, lighting candles on the dining room table. "Now run upstairs and brush your hair before dinner."

From the attic window, Josh watched the doctor's family emerging from the fog and walking toward the house. They had changed into long pants and wool sweaters. Deb was wearing lipstick the color of the hair buzzing around her face. Josh jumped down the attic stairs. "Want to see the workshop?" he asked, unlatching the front door.

While the grownups sipped drinks and ate crackers with cream cheese and cucumbers on top, Josh and

Simon took the girls to the shop. Josh wanted Deb to see Homer's castle before it got too dark.

"This is unbelievable," Wendy gasped as she stared at Simon's battleship. "How long did it take you to make this?"

"Not long," Simon said, casually.

"Look at my castle!" Josh cried, pointing to the table piled with sorted pebbles, seashells, beach glass, sea urchins, snail shells, sticks, tree bark, beach heather, and a pot of tightly covered wall plaster.

"This is REALLY cool!" Deb cried. "I especially like the crab claws on the front turret. I mean, this castle is

112

so amazing you could sell it in a store! How did you get all this stuff to stick together?"

"Just wall plaster, glue, and artistic talent," Josh said proudly. "I quit making that aircraft carrier. It had too many stupid directions. I'm better at thinking up creations on my own."

"I know exactly what you mean!" said Deb.

Wendy limped behind Simon as he led her back to the living room to eat hors-d'oeuvres. Deb and Josh stayed in the workshop. Deb wanted to make a clamshell bathtub for Homer. "I bet you never get bored on this island," Deb said as she glued two snail shells to the bottom of the white clamshell.

"In the beginning, I hated this place. I almost ran away."

"No kidding! How come you changed your mind?"

"My grandmother, mostly. I didn't want to upset her. Grumps has a fake hip and artheritis in his bones. Like I said, he's a mean, old grouch and terrible to live with. He drinks whiskey. Nana says he drinks to take away pains in his joints but I think he's addicted. Nana needs someone like me around to talk to. Besides, I get to watch the seals and work on my castle and practice rowing. I'm a good rower, you know, much better than Simon."

"How will you ever get this castle back home?"

"I'm not. I'm leaving it here. Except for all my slave labor, it's the one thing I've done on the island that old Grumps seems to like." Josh paused. "It's weird. The principal at my school says I should be a politician. Kids, even grownups, think I'm cool! I can get ANY teacher off the subject. That way they don't ask me stuff I can't answer.

"I do exactly the same thing, especially in English!"

Josh scratched his head. "Of all people, I just can't seem to win over my own grandfather. If I give him the castle, maybe he'll start to like me, at least a little."

"I bet he'll be thrilled! He's got to know how hard you've worked on it. If I was given a gift like that, I'd be grateful to that person for life."

For a minute, Josh considered giving the castle to Deb instead of his grandfather. She was *his* kind of person. She liked people and seals and mice and things in caves. He watched as Deb put a piece of green moss next to the clamshell tub. "It's a bathmat," she said.

"Come and get it!" Simon yelled as he rang the dinner bell.

In the dining room, Josh and Simon carried to the table plates heaping with spaghetti topped with

114

zucchini and steamed clams. Gramps opened a bottle of white wine. Josh had set out wine glasses for everyone, including himself.

Nana took off her glasses and untied her apron as Gramps pulled out her chair. Her cheeks were bright pink and she seemed breathless. "You kids had quite an adventure today," she said, pulling her napkin out of the silver ring.

Josh swallowed quickly so he wouldn't be talking with his mouth full. "Out on the cliffs, we heard these gunshots, so I go to Bed, 'Get back Bed! Get under the covers, I mean under cover!'"

Simon burst into giggles. "Her name is Deb, not Bed!"

"You *said* to Deb, not you *go* to Deb," Gramps corrected.

Josh clamped his arms across his chest, refusing to say another word.

"Josh was real brave," Deb continued. "He waved his shirt and shrieked at that guy in the boat. If it hadn't been for Josh, I bet he'd have killed every one of those beautiful seals. Mom, you should do a feature story on seal killers when we get back home."

"You should see what Simon and Josh are making in the workshop," Wendy said, changing the subject.

"Simon put together an awesome battleship model. Josh is making a dynamite castle out of pebbles and shells. It's even got a drawbridge hooked up with dental floss."

Gramps didn't tell Wendy that castles can't be dynamite. He didn't volunteer to be interviewed about seal killers on the 6 o'clock news. He just sipped his whiskey and sat silently at the head of the table. With strangers around, Gramps pretended to be deaf. While Nana chatted about each one of her grandchildren, he never said a word. By the time dessert was served, one of the candles had burned to a puddle of wax. Nana passed a bowl of fresh blueberries while the TV lady told stories about riding out Hurricane Bob. The doctor announced that if the fog lifted in the morning, they'd pull anchor and continue cruising up the coast.

After dinner, Gramps stood up, muttered "Good night," and limped stiffly into his bedroom, shutting the door behind him. He didn't even insist on washing the dishes. While Josh scrubbed the iron frying pan, Deb wrote her address on a scrap of paper and tucked it into the back pocket of his jeans.

"Your grandfather really is a cold fish! I want to know what he says when you give him that castle. Will you write me?"

"Ya, sure." Josh put the spaghetti pot upside down in the drying rack and borrowed her pencil. Being careful not to write with crooked letters, he spelled out the name of his street in Ledgewood, New Jersey. After checking with Simon to see if their zip code was 07450 or 07540, he handed his address to Deb.

"I'll walk you to the dock," Josh said awkwardly.

Deb brushed hair off of her face and followed Josh out the front door. In the cold, foggy darkness, Josh grabbed her hand and held it tightly.

15.

The next morning, Josh did not wake up with the chirping birds at sunrise. The night before, even after Simon had stopped reading and blown out the candles, he couldn't fall asleep. A rush of ideas crowded his brain. He imagined being interviewed by Deb's mother on nationwide TV. He'd discuss the plight of seals and how to send money to the Maine Coast Seal Protection Society to stop the senseless killings. Josh wiggled restlessly on the bumpy mattress. Thoughts of holding Deb's soft hand and touching her wild, whirling hair made him warm all over. He kicked off the quilt, feeling the sharp heart-pinch of first love.

"Eat your breakfast, dearie!" Nana gave Josh a worried look.

"I'm not hungry," Josh said, staring out at the empty harbor. "Do you have any books about seals?"

he asked, trying to make Simon think he didn't care that the doctor's boat had sailed away.

"But of course! Living on Seal Island, people have given us books about seals for years. Look on the lower shelf behind the piano."

Josh found a dusty book called *Maine Coast Marine Life*. It didn't have too many big words and there were detailed illustrations of fish, lobsters, whales, and seals. When someone banged on the front door, Josh dropped the book and raced to unlatch the door. He prayed the doctor had picked up storm warnings on his radar and returned to anchor in the harbor.

A stooped old man dressed from head to toe in yellow oilskin raingear stood at the door. His pants came up to his armpits, held up with black suspenders. He had on knee-high rubber boots and a yellow rain hat tied with worn string under his gray beard. The man's skin was as dark and wrinkled as a walnut. He smelled of dead fish.

"Hobson here?" the man asked.

"You want to see my grandfather?"

"Ayuh."

The click of the typewriter stopped and Gramps appeared at the door. "Clemer, what brings you off the boat on such a lovely day?"

"Trouble, that's what."

Gramps leaned his weight on his walking stick. "Your boat broken down?" he asked.

Clemer shook his head. "That ain't the trouble."

"You feeling sick?"

"That ain't the trouble neither. We got us a minke in distress. She's drifting off the south shore."

"What's a minke?" Josh asked.

Gramps stroked his prickly chin whiskers. "A minke is a whale," he replied.

"Tried to push her out to sea with the boat, but she come back in on the tide. Must be sick or maybe dead."

Gramps put his hand on Josh's shoulder. "Go tell Rosie I'm going out on the boat with Clemer. No telling when I'll be back."

"Can I come too?" Josh pleaded. "I've wanted to see a whale since I was a little kid!"

"Get your life jacket and meet us on the dock," Gramps said.

Josh tiptoed past Simon reading in the hammock. Even if he had to spend time with old bug-eyes, it would be worth it to see a whale. If Simon went along, he'd spend the whole time bragging about his knowledge of whales. Simon thought he knew everything.

Clemer's lobster boat stank of dead fish bait. Josh wanted to hold his nose. Afraid of hurting Clemer's feelings, he stood in the wind where the smell wasn't quite so sickening.

"Mind if I pull a few traps on the way?" Clemer pointed his boat into the wind and slowed the motor. Leaning overboard, he grabbed the handle of a bobbing orange and green buoy. He threw the buoy into the boat and put the dripping rope around the winch. "In the old days we had to haul the traps by hand. Now this here winch pulls most of the weight." Bending over the side of the boat, Clemer hoisted the dripping wire trap onto the side rail of his boat. Inside the wire cage, Josh saw two lobsters, a bunch of crabs, and a fish.

"Too small?" Gramps pointed at one of the lobsters.

Clemer grabbed the lobster in his heavy glove. With a metal stick, he measured the lobster from its beady eyes to the end of its back. "Ayah," he said, throwing the lobster back into the ocean. "Spend my day sorting the keepers from the shorts," he said scratching his nose with the giant glove. "Used to peg the cruncher claw. Now we band 'em." Clemer wrapped a second rubber band around the scissor claw of the keeper. "Reason being to keep 'em from biting each other. Good thing is, if a lobsta loses a leg or a claw, nature grows it back."

"How many traps do you have?" Josh asked.

"Used to have 200. Now I got 'bout 100." Clemer refilled the wire net with bait, a stinking fish head covered with black flies. Then he dropped the trap over the side of the boat. The bricks on the bottom of the cage made it sink quickly to the ocean floor.

"How come you wanted to be a lobsterman?" Josh asked.

Clemer bent over the side of the boat and grabbed another orange and green buoy. "Folks say all ya need to lobsta is a weak mind and a strong back. I ain't never had a boss though, never in my life, 'cept for the old lady, and when I was in the Navy. I aim to keep it that way."

Clemer's boat, the *Betty Ann,* got smacked by another wave. Josh blinked stinging salt spray out of his eyes. He could think of better ways to be self-employed. You could play in a rock band or be a mystery writer or invent Nintendo computer games. That way you'd never have to worry about gale winds, falling overboard, getting lost in fog, or turning lonely.

Josh watched the green-brown lobsters in the wooden crate, their two feelers wiggling wildly. He wanted to rip the rubber bands off the claws and throw the trapped creatures back into the sea. He'd eaten a cooked red lobster when they'd come to Maine for Nana's seventy-fifth birthday. He doubted he'd ever want to eat lobster again.

Clemer steered the *Betty Ann* around the south end of the island. Josh could see patches of cattails growing in the marsh along the shore. They looked like hundreds of hot dogs waving on giant sticks. In the distance, he spotted a fifteen-foot black hill on the beach.

Clemer slowed the boat's motor. "Thar she blows!"

"Sure is a big fellow," Gramps said. "Wonder what made it come ashore like that?"

"I know!" Josh cried. "I bet it got shot! I bet that crazy guy in the lobster boat picked off this whale just like he murdered my seals. Maybe it's not really dead, just wounded," he said hopefully.

Clemer shook his head. "She's a goner," he said simply.

"NOW can we call the Coast Guard?" Josh asked his grandfather. "This is turning into a war!"

Gramps shook his head. "Nothing the Coast Guard can do about it now," he said. "We've got a bigger problem."

"Bigger than capturing killers?" Josh cried.

"Ayuh," Clemer said. "Your grandpa is right. We got us a real big problem."

"What? More killings? Think they'll turn their guns on us?"

"Ain't people that's the problem," Clemer said.

"So what is it then?" Josh asked impatiently.

"Stench! Half a ton of rotting minke."

Josh tried to remember how many pounds there were in a ton. One thing for sure: if he thought he'd puke at the smell of a few pounds of dead herring bait, the stink of a decomposing whale was beyond imagination.

16.

The next day after lunch, Josh lay on his bed reading about whales. The *Maine Coast Marine Life* book said that whales could live to be sixty years old and spend up to two hours underwater. Josh wanted to quiz Simon on whale facts, but Simon was reading his tenth book in the hammock.

Josh heard the low drone of a boat's motor in the harbor. Clemer pulled traps from 5:30 a.m. until 2:00 p.m. Then he went home and took a nap. Clemer had promised to help Gramps with the beached whale. If the huge carcass did not drift out to sea on the high tide, they'd have no choice. They'd have to burn it. Clemer said Bart and Franklin and his sons, Wayne and Lester, would come over to lend a hand after they finished hauling for the day.

Gramps tapped the barometer. "It looks like a good day for burning," he reported. "The wind will blow the stench out to sea."

"Is Clemer picking us up in the lobster boat?" Josh asked.

"The *Betty Ann* draws too much water. She'll have to anchor off shore. We'll need the dory to get Clemer and the other men from the boat to the beach."

"Can I row?"

Gramps shook his head. "I doubt you can handle the weight."

"I'm coming too," Simon interrupted. Josh could tell his brother was annoyed he'd missed the trip in Clemer's lobster boat yesterday.

"You walk," Gramps said.

"Okey-dokey," Simon muttered.

Nana called from the kitchen, "I think I'll come along too."

"This is no work for a woman, Rosie," Gramps replied.

"I'm as tough as any man, and you know it," Nana called back in a cross voice. "Besides, I want to talk to Franklin. His wife has been ailing ever since Wayne's wife ran off with the well digger from up north. Imagine being sick and trying to take care of all those kids. Poor woman. There's been so much tragedy in that family."

"I'll ask Franklin about his wife," Josh said. Secretly, he wished his grandmother was coming along. If she were in the boat, he wouldn't have to talk to Grumps. Nana could tell stories about Franklin's tragedies and the run-away romance with the well digger.

Nana tied her straw hat under her sagging chin. "Lunch is in the picnic basket," she said coldly, picking up her painting easel.

While Simon set off around the island on foot, Josh helped his grandfather load the picnic lunch, buckets of kindling wood, fire logs, and two tins of kerosene into the dory. "I've gotten a lot stronger," Josh said, flexing his muscles as he slipped his arm into the red life jacket. "See, I even got calluses on my hands from rowing!"

"You are a determined lad. Take the oars!" Gramps grunted as he sat in the stern of the row boat. Josh sat down on the middle seat. He put the oars in the oarlocks and pulled hard on the right oar. The dory glided away from the dock. Josh dipped the oars in and out of the water with a confident, steady rhythm.

Halfway around the island, there was a sudden flutter of wings and loud cackling sounds. Birds as large as hawks circled protectively in the sky. "Nesting ospreys," Gramps said. "The nesting Arctic terns have already departed. They migrate across the Atlantic to the Arctic Circle. By the time those birds return to Seal Island next spring, they'll have flown some 22,000 miles."

"That's a mighty long way to fly!" Josh ducked as a bird swooped down and tried to dive bomb the boat.

"Row faster," Gramps ordered, putting on his hat.

Josh rowed with all his might. He pretended he was in a horror movie, escaping starving black vultures. The boat skimmed along the water. As they got farther away from the nesting place, the shrieking cries changed to an occasional squawk.

"A *fratercula arctica!*" Gramps pointed his hairy finger. "That's the Latin name for the Arctic puffin. At the turn of the century, puffin feathers were used on ladies' fancy hats. They killed off those unfortunate birds by the thousands."

Josh looked over his shoulder. In a cove at the southern tip of the island, he saw the black back of the whale rising from the rocky beach. In the distance, he heard another wave of shrieking birds, sounding calls of alarm.

"Simon must be walking past the nesting place," Gramps said.

Josh beached the dory and helped his grandfather out of the stern. Suddenly Simon came running around the point. "Those birds tried to KILL me!" he panted.

Josh grinned. "You've got bird doo-doo in your hair!"

"Oh, gross! And I can't even take a shower!"

Gramps handed Simon his handkerchief. "Help your brother collect driftwood. We'll need all the kindling we can find to burn a whale of this bulk."

After collecting piles of washed-up logs and dead branches, Simon sat on a rock and started to read. Josh walked along the shoreline to search for more dried sticks. He saw Gramps limping toward him. He was carrying an armful of driftwood and waving a glass bottle.

"COOL!" cried Josh. "It's got a message inside!" Josh uncorked the bottle and used a twig to fish out a tightly rolled note. "Want some fun in Port Clyde?" he read aloud. "Call Angie at 372-2918 for a night to remember!"

Simon grabbed the bottle. "Let me see that!"

"That bottle belongs to Joshua."

"Gee, thanks, Gramps!" Josh sat on a rock and read the note again. Simon opened the picnic basket and took out a tuna sandwich and the largest piece of blueberry pie.

"Looks like the *Betty Ann*." Gramps gulped lemonade from the thermos bottle. He cupped his hand over his eyes and pointed.

Josh quickly finished his pie and jumped into the dory. He rowed out to the deep water where Clemer had anchored the lobster boat. "How long will it take to burn the whale?" Josh asked as he rowed Clemer, Franklin, and his two sons back to the shore.

"'B'out four to six hours," Franklin said, "if she's the same size as the minke we burned on Fog Island two years ago. This your first burning, kid?"

Josh nodded.

"Hope you got a strong stomach."

"Sure do," said Josh, already feeling sick.

The men surrounded the whale carcass with the fire logs, driftwood, and dry branches. Josh could tell that his grandfather and the lobstermen were old friends. Even though they didn't talk much, he felt their sense of trust. Bart walked around the whale, dousing the logs with kerosene. "Got a match, Clemer?" he called.

"Ayuh." Clemer took a pipe and then a box of kitchen matches from the pocket of his oilskin overalls. He struck a match. The fire logs and dried sticks immediately burst into a roaring blaze. As the whale's skin burned, oily blubber flared up in black smoke, sending a sickening rancid smell into the air.

Simon paced back and forth in front of the marsh grass at the top of the rocky beach. He had filled the buckets with salt water in case of blowing sparks. He pinched his nose closed with two fingers and breathed through his mouth. "Get me out of here!" he moaned in a nasal voice. "It stinks to high heaven."

"Wind is shifting to the south." Gramps threw more driftwood on the fire. "This stench will be all over the island in no time."

"Ayuh," Bart agreed.

Josh stared at the burning whale. He swallowed hard. Tears from smoke and heat and anger filled his eyes. What could have killed such a magnificent creature? The sickening feeling in the pit of his stomach reminded Josh of the day his dog got hit by a Jeep on Main Street. "You think that whale died of old age?" he asked Clemer.

"Doubt it," Clemer replied, stepping back from the flames. The heat from the fire had begun to melt his rubber boots.

"How's your wife doing?" Josh asked Franklin.

"She ain't doin' too good," he replied, walking away.

Josh wanted to ask Wayne about his run-away wife but the fishy fumes of the burning whale made him feel nauseous. He tied a napkin from the picnic basket over his nose. He didn't care if he looked silly. It was better than puking up his lunch.

After what seemed like ten hours, only the whale's smoldering bones were left on the beach. Josh held his nose and picked up the minke's jaw bone and teeth. The men doused the fire with buckets of salt water and wrapped the skeleton with heavy rope. Wayne held onto the rope as Josh rowed the lobstermen out to the *Betty Ann*. Tying the rope to a cleat on the stern of the lobster boat, Clemer revved the engine. The *Betty Ann* slowly dragged the whale's carcass down the beach and into the sea.

With the checkered napkin still knotted around the back of his head, Josh thanked Clemer and his friends for their help.

"Always thaya if you need me," Clemer mumbled.

Josh rowed the dory back to the shore. Simon loaded the buckets, empty kerosene tins, whale jaw, and message bottle into the boat. "Get me out of here, Bro!" he moaned in a weak voice.

Josh gagged from the stink of burning whale as he rowed back toward the harbor. With the wind shift, the dory bobbed up and down in the choppy, white-capped waves. Even so, he never lost control of the oars. Gramps sat in the stern, watching Josh's every stroke. Simon sat limply in the bow of the boat, as white as a clamshell. When a marsh hawk flew over the boat, he didn't even mark the sighting in his nature notebook.

"Thanks for the ride, young man." Gramps put the dory painter between his teeth and slowly climbed the dock ladder. Josh kept the dory from banging against the dock while his grandfather tied a clove hitch to the post. "Pack your things," Gramps said. "With the wind change, we'll spend the night in Moxie Cove. Even Rosie can't sleep with a stench like this."

It was so dark on the trip ashore, Gramps had to navigate by compass and the light of the moon. When they got to the shore house, Josh decided he would let Simon shower first. The bird poop had hardened in his hair. The thought of turning on an electric light, watching TV, or calling Angie in Port Clyde kept Josh from focusing on the smelly air and rolling ocean waves.

Josh hoped he'd get a postcard from his parents and a long letter from Zipper. If there was time, he'd pick up a few books on whales at the Moxie Cove Library. He imagined bringing the whale's jaw to homeroom the first day of school. No one else at the Valley Middle School would own a whale's jaw with two perfect rows of teeth. No one else would have a washed-up bottle with a message from a girl, no one but him.

17.

After a quick food shop, the next stop in Moxie Cove was a trip to the post office. In the mail there were two boring postcards from England. Josh wanted to see pictures of dungeons and gallows, not the royal family. Zipper had sent a letter. He said the Valley Vulture All Stars had lost the championship to the Paramus Pirates. Since the end of the baseball season, he'd played drums and Nintendo all day because life in New Jersey was so boring. He wished he could be on an island watching live seals and searching for treasure in a cave.

At the winter house everyone took a shower to wash whale soot out of their hair. Nana did two loads of laundry. After supper, Josh tore a sheet of paper from the grocery list pad. He printed in his best handwriting, "Deer Deb." He proofread carefully to make sure he had written Deb instead of Bed. It was hard to write to a girl when you worried about your spelling. Deb would know how to sound out his words about the burning of the whale. She'd understand what he meant.

The next morning, Gramps pounded his fist on the guest room door. "Time to get moving," he announced.

Simon woke with a start and squinted at his watch. "But it's quarter to five in the morning!"

"Tide's going out."

Josh rolled over in bed. He knew the *Odyssey* needed at least thirty inches of water to land at the big dock; otherwise, they'd have to unload at the drain tide dock and drag all the supplies over the mud flats to shore. It was the tide, daylight, and hunger that governed life on an island. You didn't really need a watch.

Gramps stood at the wheel and steered the *Odyssey* through the maze of shoals and lobster buoys. Josh spotted three of Clemer's orange and green buoys bobbing in the water. The sun sparkled on the waves as the boat turned into the harbor. With a fresh coat of blue paint on the front door, and the broken shutter fixed, the old house looked more like a real home. Taking a deep breath, Josh detected only the slightest trace of dead whale smell in the air.

Josh lugged a heavy canvas bag of groceries up the dock ladder. After helping Nana put away the supplies, he ran up the attic stairs and presented Homer with a piece of parmesan cheese. "Your mouse castle is almost ready!" he said in a high, sing-song voice, the kind of voice his mother used to speak to babies. "I just need to glue more snail shells to the turrets. After I tie the crab claws together to hold the flag, your deluxe habitat will be complete!"

Josh ran downstairs to the workshop. He stood for a moment to admire his creation. There was a dried starfish crest on the castle door. The dental floss tied to the drawbridge moved it up and down over the birch bark moat. A scallop shell stairway led to all four turrets. The plastered rock and pebble walls were so thick that Homer couldn't gnaw his way out.

Josh planned to take pictures of the castle from every angle to show Zipper and his mom and dad. This was the best project he'd ever invented. Even Gramps would be impressed. He'd probably keep the castle in his study, next to the typewriter.

Simon came to the dining room table for lunch with a book in his hand. Nana made him put it away while he ate. Gramps sat down at the head of the table. "Something is wrong," he sighed, as he pulled his cloth napkin out of the silver napkin ring.

"What is it, Hobs? Don't you feel well?"

"It's not me, Rosie. Something is wrong with my typewriter. Ever since we spent the night ashore, the letter "k" won't print."

"You've had that typewriter for over forty years. Maybe it's just worn out."

Gramps took a sip of cold carrot soup. "It's squeaking, Rosie. My typewriter has never squeaked before."

"After lunch I'll take a look at it," Josh said. "I'm good at fixing stuff. Once I fixed the toilet and I figured out how to get Mom's computer printer to work."

"I'd take a typewriter over a computer any day, even if it never prints another "k" again."

"Computer technology is the wave of the future, Gramps. Don't you want to be right up there with all the other scholars?" Simon asked.

Nana dipped her spoon into the soup. "You boys must have computers at school."

The word "school" made Josh cringe. More than half the summer was over. He dreaded starting sixth grade in the big middle school. Hanging out with his friends, playing fall soccer, and taking hot showers in a real bathroom was all he had to look forward to. Even computer class was confusing, unless he sat next to Zipper. Zipper was a brain. He could do everything. He even knew how to play cymbals and the drums.

After lunch, Josh followed his grandfather to his desk. "This typewriter is a real antique," he said, turning it upside down. "I need a screwdriver."

Gramps fumbled through his top desk drawer and pulled out an old Swiss Army knife. Opening one of the blades, he handed Josh a tiny screwdriver.

"I see what you mean about the squeaking," Josh said. Carefully he unscrewed the top cover of the typewriter. Inside he saw two beady, black eyes staring up at him. A mouse sat quivering in the nest of keys, its tail firmly jammed between the "k" and the "j." Josh took the screwdriver and freed the terrified creature. It leapt off the desk and ran into the bathroom.

"Excellent!" Gramps chuckled, patting Josh on the shoulder. "You do have a decided knack for fixing things. After my afternoon siesta, we'll continue the repairs on the drain tide dock."

Josh walked out of the room. "No way!" he mumbled under his breath. Even though Grumps was acting a little more human, he felt he'd earned an afternoon off, especially after the trauma of the whale burning. Rebuilding the drain tide dock was right up there with roof repair and chimney cleaning on his list of most hated projects. He had much better ways to spend the afternoon. Besides, Simon never really helped. He just stood around and complained.

Josh heard snoring coming from his grandparents' bedroom. Tiptoeing past the door, he carried Homer in the birdcage through the storage room and into the workshop. The house was quiet. Simon was reading in the hammock and Nana had walked to the other end of the island to work on her painting of the eagle's nest.

Josh dropped Homer by the tail into the castle. Homer stood still. He wiggled his whiskers and then scurried around in circles. Josh filled Deb's clam shell bathtub with drinking water and crumbled a trail of cookie crumbs from the round rock table to all four turrets. Homer leapt up the shell staircase and nibbled at the crumbs. Josh could tell that he was thrilled by his royal rodent habitat.

After taking a few photographs of Homer in the mouse castle, Josh set an old window screen over the turrets so that Homer could not escape. Slinging Simon's camera over his shoulder, he walked along the forest path to the cliffs. He wanted to send Deb photos of the castle and Flipper. She'd be relieved to know that the seal pup had survived the lobsterman's attack.

On the way back from the cliffs, Josh stepped off the trail and picked handfuls of wild raspberries. If he stayed away until 4 o'clock when Gramps had his afternoon tea, it would be too late to start fixing the dock.

When Josh finally got back to the house, Simon was nowhere in sight. Josh grabbed his book about whales and stretched out in the hammock. He opened the book at his feather place-mark. As he began to read, he heard a faint cry. It sounded like a sick seagull. Josh kept on reading until he heard the cry again. This time he stopped swinging and lay still in the hammock. He could make out the sound of a very weak voice. It seemed to be calling, "Help! Help! Someone help me!"

18.

Josh dropped his book and jumped out of the hammock. He cupped his ear and listened. Along with the squawk of the gulls and the flapping of the American flag, he definitely heard the cry of a human voice.

Josh looked toward the harbor. He couldn't see anyone. Perhaps Simon was calling for help. Maybe Simon had walked back to examine the osprey's nests and had been attacked. Josh looked toward the south end of the island. The sky was clear. No squawking birds rose in a protective army around their nesting young.

The wind could carry the sound of a lobsterman's radio to shore. Josh scanned the horizon. There were no lobster boats in sight. This late in the afternoon, the lobstermen would be selling the day's catch to restaurants full of hungry tourists wearing lobster bibs.

Josh picked up his book and climbed back into the hammock. Maybe the call for help was just in his imagination. Once, by the cliffs, a bird's call had sounded so much like a human voice he thought he was being followed by a stranger. Swaying back and forth in the hammock, Josh closed his eyes. He imagined his grandfather's amazed look of pride as he presented him the castle.

"Help me, for God's sake, someone help me!"

Josh opened his eyes. Birds didn't talk about God. The faint cry HAD to be the voice of a person! Josh jumped back out of the hammock. Afraid of stepping on a bee in the clover, he quickly put on his sneakers and tied the laces.

"Where are you?" Josh yelled, running full speed down the grass path in the direction of the water.

"Over here," a weak voice called. "On the drain tide dock."

With a shudder of horror, Josh saw his grandfather's twisted body lying on the seaweed-covered rocks. Without stopping to take off his sneakers, he ran over the mud flats and into the shallow water.

"What happened?" Josh called. "Are you all right?"

"No! I am not all right," Gramps said weakly.

Josh bent over his grandfather. He grabbed his arms and tried to sit him up.

"Don't! Don't touch me!" he moaned. "I'm paralyzed. I can't move."

"What happened?" Josh panted. He watched the waves lapping at his grandfather's limp body.

"I slipped piling rocks on the dock. I think my hip has come out of the socket. The pain is excruciating."

"I'll get help. I'll go find Simon and Nana."

"No time," Gramps whispered in a dry, thin voice. Josh could see his teeth were chattering. "Tide is coming in. Hypothermia," he moaned.

Josh didn't know what hypothermia was but he knew it sounded bad. One thing for sure, if he left his grandfather on the rocks much longer, the rising tide would cover his body with freezing seawater.

"I'll go get the boat and row you ashore."

"Can't get in the boat," his grandfather sputtered.

"Then I'll carry you ashore. I can pull you by the arms."

Gramps shook his head. "Too far. Too heavy. Can't move."

A sudden calm crossed Gramps's face. He turned sheet-white and closed his eyes.

"Oh my God," Josh yelled out loud. "He's dead!"

Picking up his grandfather's limp arm, Josh felt for a pulse. He tried to remember everything Scout Master Holmes had said about lifesaving. He'd practiced giving the Heimlich maneuver. He wished his grandfather was choking instead of drowning. That way he'd know exactly what to do.

Josh felt a weak heartbeat. "He's not dead!" he whispered. He remembered the TV episode of *Emergency Squad* when a man lost consciousness because he went into shock. The medics had wrapped the man in a blanket.

"I'll be right back!" Josh yelled in his grandfather's ear, just in case he could hear him. He waded through water up to his knees and over the mud flats. By the time he got to the sandy beach, he could barely feel his feet. His toes were numb with cold.

"HELP!" Josh yelled as he raced up the path to the house. He knew that Nana was painting on the other side of the island. She would never hear his voice. Josh screamed for his brother as he unlatched the front door. There was no reply.

Josh rushed into his grandparents' room and grabbed the blanket off the double bed. Standing stone still beside his grandfather's typewriter, he felt his heart pounding out of control. What use was a blanket if it got sopping wet?

Repeating over and over, "Stay calm, don't panic, stay calm, don't panic," Josh raced into the kitchen. He reached for the cell phone on the top shelf and dialed 1-119-SOS-HELP. A voice at the other end of the line said, "Your call cannot be completed as dialed." In frustration, Josh stuffed the telephone in his back pocket and grabbed the dinner bell from the kitchen shelf. He ran outside by the wild rose bushes and swung the bell wildly.

Josh looked frantically toward the water. He could see his grandfather, crumpled like a broken string puppet on the drain tide dock. How could he rescue him if he couldn't lift his body into a boat? Suddenly the image of Homer floating on a raft through the castle moat flashed into his brain. If he could roll his grandfather's body onto something flat, he could float him safely to shore.

Josh flung open the door to his grandfather's workshop. Desperately, his eyes scanned the cluttered room. Josh stared at his worktable. He grabbed Simon's battleship off the hollow door and laid it carefully on a wooden crate. Then he put his arms around the castle. As he lifted it up, the bottom fell out. The four walls of the

castle cracked and broke, falling with a crash into a pile
of rocks, shells, and crumbled plaster. Homer leapt over
a turret and escaped behind a stack of empty paint cans.

Josh stared at his ruined castle. Tears burned his
eyes. He counted to ten, blew his nose on a corner of
the bed blanket, and dragged the wooden door out of
the workshop. Josh found the wheelbarrow under a tree
near the vegetable garden. He balanced the door and

blanket on top of the wheelbarrow and raced down the bumpy grass path to the beach.

With all his strength, Josh pulled the door across the mud flats. When he got to ripples of the incoming tide, he floated the door to the drain tide dock. By the time he reached his grandfather, the water was lapping around his limp body. Josh rolled his grandfather off the drain tide dock and onto the floating door. Gramps groaned but didn't speak. His lips had turned navy blue.

19.

Simon raced down the beach, waving his book. "What happened? What did you do to Gramps?" Simon stared at the limp body lying on the worktable, wrapped tightly in a pink bed blanket. He helped Josh tug the heavy door over the mud flats toward the beach.

Josh stroked his grandfather's cold hand. "I was reading in the hammock and I heard this cry. I thought it was some sort of bird. Then I saw Gramps lying on the drain tide dock. His legs looked all weird. I tried to pull him off the dock but he kept saying, 'Don't touch me!' He said he couldn't move because his hip got messed up and he had hypermania."

"So why is he lying on our worktable?" Simon asked, pacing back and forth in the mud. "What are we going to do now?"

"The tide was coming in and Gramps's lips were purple and his head was sitting in a puddle. I rolled him off the rocks onto the worktable. Then I floated him to shore. Lucky you came along. The door was too heavy to pull up the mud flats by myself."

"I'll go get the first aid book in the bathroom," Simon said. "It will show how to do artificial respiration."

"But he didn't swallow water. He just got in shock from pain and cold, like that guy on *Emergency Squad*"

"I'll go find Nana. She'll know what to do." Simon said in a quick, panicky voice.

"There isn't time, Simon. We've got to get Gramps to a hostipal. I called the Coast Guard but they didn't answer." Josh took the cell phone out of his back pocket and handed it to his brother.

"Here, you try," he said.

"What's the number?"

"Dial 1-119-SOS-HELP"

"That's not how you do it!" Simon yelled. "You dial 911, not 119." He punched in the numbers and held the phone to his ear. "It's ringing!"

Josh grabbed the telephone out of his brother's hand. "Emergency!" he yelled into the phone. "Send a chopper to Seal Island. Hobson Wilkes has fallen and replaced his hip. He's in shock with hypermania and he can't talk."

"What are they saying?" Simon asked, pacing back and forth.

"They want to speak to an adult," Josh whispered.

"Oh my God, they won't come! They won't help us," Simon groaned. "He's going to die. I just know it. Gramps is going to die!"

Josh took a deep breath. In a calm, firm voice, he said, "You can't speak to my grandmother because she's at the other end of the island painting a picture. Me and my brother are with Gramps. I floated him off the drain tide dock before he got covered with water. Right now he's lying on a door on the mud flats wrapped in a blanket. His lips are purple but he's breathing."

"They want directions!" Josh whispered excitedly. "Tell them how to get to Seal Island."

Simon grabbed the phone. "From Moxie Cove, fly east over Cranberry and Fog Islands. Then you go over ocean for about two more miles. From the dock in Moxie Cove, Seal Island is four miles out to sea." There was a pause. "They see Seal on the chart!" Simon cried. "The lady is sending a helicopter to take Gramps to Miles Memorial Hospital."

Josh took the cell phone from his brother. His voice was calm. "Go get the first aid book," he said. "I'll stay here with Gramps."

Simon raced over the mud flats toward the house. He returned waving the book with a red cross on the front. "What happened to your castle?" he panted. "It's ruined!"

"Don't remind me," Josh said. "Quick! Look up 'Going into Shock.'"

"That's not how it's listed," Simon said, running his finger down the index until he got to the word "shock." "Put something under Gramps's feet. The book says the feet should be raised thirty centimeters so the blood will flow from the legs to the upper body."

Josh ran to the beach and lugged back a rock. "How much is thirty centimeters?" he asked, propping his grandfather's feet on the stone.

"About a foot. Now we need to loosen his clothing and keep the body warm while we wait for professional medical attention."

"He's sweating but his skin is cold," Josh said.

"Maybe we should take off the blanket," Simon suggested.

"No way! On *Emergency Squad* they said to keep the body warm." Josh tucked the blanket under his grandfather's chin. "Give me your baseball hat. Body heat escapes out the top of your head." Josh lifted his grandfather's head and slipped Simon's Yankee cap on his head. He saw his grandfather's eyes flutter beneath his bushy eyebrows.

"Don't bring me back," he muttered. "Let me stay home."

"What's he talking about?" Simon asked.

Josh shrugged his shoulders. "How should I know? At least he's talking!" He bent over his grandfather and whispered in his ear, "Don't worry Gramps. Help is on the way."

Josh rubbed his grandfather's arms and legs to keep the circulation moving while Simon read aloud about medical emergencies from the First Aid book. It seemed like hours had passed before they spotted a helicopter whirling toward the island. The faint drone of its motor turned into a deafening roar. The helicopter circled the island and landed in the meadow behind the house. People carrying a stretcher came racing down the grass path toward the beach. One man took Gramps's pulse while a woman listened to his chest.

"He's got a strong heart," the lady said reassuringly.

The medics lifted Gramps off the door, strapped him onto the stretcher, and rushed him up the path to the waiting helicopter.

"Can I come too?" Josh yelled over the roar of the whirling blades. "Is Gramps going to be OK?"

The woman doctor handed Josh a clipboard. "Sign on this line," she said, pointing to a form.

Josh grabbed a pen out of Simon's shirt pocket and wrote "Joshua Grant" in cursive writing.

The woman gave Josh a duplicate copy of the form and hooked the clipboard to the end of the stretcher. "You and your brother need to stay on the island and look after your grandmother," she said. "I know old Hobson Wilkes. He taught my brothers Latin at the University. Rosie works on the church altar guild with my mother." Pointing to the hospital letterhead on the form, she said, "Call this number in four hours. By then we'll have a better prognosis."

Josh clutched the paper tightly so the swirling winds from the rotating blades wouldn't blow it out of his hand. He gave a quick wave as the helicopter rose back up into the sky.

As the boys ran through the tall field grass back to the house, they saw their grandmother in her floppy straw hat hurrying out of the woods. She had her paint box in one hand and the canvas in the other.

"My lands! I never heard so much noise," she exclaimed. "Someone should tell those helicopter pilots not to fly so low over the islands."

"Nana, the helicopter landed here," Josh said gently. "It came to get Gramps. He took a little spill on the drain tide dock and we thought he should see a doctor."

Nana dropped the paint box and canvas on the ground. "You mean Hobs flew off in that thing?" she gasped, looking up in the sky. "He HATES to fly! When's he coming back?"

"He'll come back as soon as he gets fixed up." Josh put his arm around his grandmother's waist. "We have a number to call after supper to see how he's doing. The doctor lady even knows you from church and Gramps taught her brothers Latin."

"That must be Bonnie Blodget from Waldoboro. I remember the day she got accepted to medical school." Nana picked up her paint box and canvas. "I've never spent a night on Seal Island without Hobs," she said, staring up at the sky in stunned disbelief.

20.

Without Gramps, the familiar routines of the household seemed oddly out of step. Josh found himself tapping the barometer and announcing the temperature each morning. Nana no longer bothered to cook hot oatmeal for breakfast. She read a new book, *Robinson Crusoe,* both before lunch and by candlelight after dinner. She said reading out loud kept her mind from worrying.

The doctors at the hospital reported that Hobson Wilkes was making a satisfactory recovery, for a man his age. The x-rays had shown that his artificial hip had come out of the socket. Under anesthesia, they had put it back in place. There was no need for further surgery. Even so, Dr. Gardner wanted to keep his patient in the hospital for several days of observation.

Nana called the hospital three times a day. She carried the cell phone around the house in the pocket of her apron. "It keeps me closer to Hobs," she said. When she called her daughter Rachel in Boston, Josh didn't want to talk to his cousins. He knew the accident had been his fault. Simon told Katie, Sam, and baby Willy all about Gramps getting airlifted off Seal Island. Rachel said that when she had surgery, the anesthesia made her feel groggy for weeks. She warned that Gramps wouldn't be the same when he returned to the island.

"When are you going to call Mom and Dad?" Josh asked.

"No use upsetting people on vacation," Nana sighed. "Besides, Hobs would holler if I used this phone to call overseas. Just imagine the expense!"

Josh washed the pink blanket from his grandparents' bed in the kitchen sink. He hung it over tomato posts in the garden to dry. Then he scrubbed the muddy door with a wire brush and a bucket of salt water. Simon helped him lift the worktable back into place in Gramps's shop.

"You going to rebuild that castle?" Simon asked.

"It's no use," Josh said as he swept crumbled pieces of plaster, rocks, and the clamshell bathtub into the dust pan. "Besides, Homer escaped."

"That's a real bummer, Bro. You worked real hard on that thing. I'm giving my battleship to Gramps as a get well present." Simon took a tiny brush and painted a yellow waterline along the hull of the ship. "Just like I said, when you follow the directions exactly, your model turns out just perfect!"

Josh knew he could never measure up to Simon, not in his grandfather's eyes. Even if he'd given him Homer's castle, he'd probably have hidden it away in a trunk in the attic or taken it to the dump in Moxie Cove.

In the afternoons, while Simon worked on his model or read in the hammock, Josh walked along the shore, collecting flat rocks. When the tide was low, he loaded the rocks into the dory and rowed them to the drain tide dock. He wore his grandfather's knee-high rubber boots over his sneakers to keep his feet from freezing.

Straining every muscle in his body to lift the rocks, Josh felt momentary relief from the gusts of guilt that swirled in his head. If only he'd helped his grandfather repair the dock instead of sneaking off to the cliffs, it never would have happened. He could have broken his grandfather's fall and carried him to safety. He could have saved him from the terror of the lapping, incoming tide. Josh knew that Gramps had never really liked him. Now he had every reason to HATE him for the rest of his life!

At night, Nana read aloud the final chapters of *Robinson Crusoe*. She read more than one chapter at a time. No one wanted to leave the cozy living room. Josh dreaded going to bed. Exhausted as he was from lifting rocks, he tossed at night with tortured, terrible dreams.

"You think Gramps will be coming back soon?" Simon yawned. "I've got a surprise for him."

"Dr. Gardner thinks Hobs may be released as early as tomorrow morning. I imagine they'll be mighty happy to get rid of him. He's been complaining something awful about being cooped up in a hospital bed."

"Believe it or not, I really miss old Gramps," Simon said.

Nana blew out the candles on the table next to her reading chair. "Me too," she sighed. "Never realized how much I loved the old coot 'til he wasn't here."

Josh carried a candle up the attic stairs to brush his teeth. He didn't miss his grandfather one bit. He dreaded the moment he'd have to confront the old man, face to face. Before he climbed under the quilt, Josh crossed off another day on the calendar. Only two more days until his parents returned from England. If Gramps was still in the hospital, Josh wondered how they'd get ashore. Four miles was a mighty long way to row.

Josh woke up at dawn the next morning. Even before opening his eyes, he could tell by the chilly, humid dampness that sheets of fog were blowing through the window screen. With a sense of relief, he realized that Gramps would be forced to stay in the hospital another day. Even Clemer wouldn't go out in a fog so thick that you couldn't see the rose bushes.

Josh rolled over in bed. He checked to see if Homer had returned to curl up under the chewed-up socks. The cookie crumbs were gone, but the birdcage was empty. Homer must be sleeping with his family behind the attic walls. Josh thought about his own family. He'd be happy to see his parents. He'd be even happier to see Zipper and his friends in school. The homesick pain he'd felt the first weeks on the island had gone away. He'd proven to himself that he could make it on his own, even living with Simon and his bug-eyed grandfather.

As Josh opened his book to the chapter on whales, he heard the faint putt-putt of a lobster boat in the harbor. His heart sank. "Simon, wake up," he said. "I think I hear Clemer's boat."

Simon opened one eye and looked out the window. "You must be hearing things, Bro. It's too foggy."

Josh grabbed jeans and a shirt off the floor, got dressed, and ran down the attic stairs. He found Nana cooking oatmeal in the kitchen. She was wearing pearls and bright red lipstick. Josh saw the cell phone sticking out of the pocket of her wrinkled blue dress.

"Dr. Gardner released Hobs!" she cried, peering out the window. "I hope he didn't badger Clemer into bringing him out to the island on a day like this."

Josh was swallowing his vitamin pill when the door latch opened. Gramps hobbled into the living room, followed by Clemer.

"Hobson!" Nana cried. With eyes closed, she swayed back and forth in her husband's outstretched arms.

Clemer looked away. "Thick o' fog out theyah," he said to Josh. "Had to use the compass all the way from Moxie Cove."

With one arm still around his wife, Hobson pointed a hairy finger at Josh. "That's the one," he said to Clemer in a shaky voice.

Josh felt his heart thumping. His palms broke out in a sticky sweat. His empty stomach knotted in a rush of guilt and fear. He wanted to race outside and hide deep in the pine forest.

"That's the boy who . . ."

"Gramps, I'm REALLY sorry, I . . ."

"That's the boy who saved my life!"

Josh caught his breath. He stared wide-eyed at his grandfather.

"I know what you did, young man," he said. "You kept a level head. You didn't panic. No question about it, Joshua, you saved me from drowning."

"But I thought you were unconscientious," Josh stammered.

Grandfather's pinched lips curled into a smile. "While I may have appeared unconscious, I remember everything. What happened to me on those rocks has changed my life. I've got quite a story to tell you," he said, sinking into the chair at the head of the table.

Clemer took a step toward the front door.

"Are you leaving?" Rosie asked.

"Ayuh. Heard the story twice," he said. "Brought you four lobstas." Clemer put a dripping plastic bag into the kitchen sink.

"Won't you join us for coffee until the fog burns off?"

"Got to get back to the *Betty Ann.*"

"Thanks again for your help, Clemer." Gramps winced as he moved his leg. "You need anything, you know who to come to."

"Ayuh," Clemer nodded. He opened the front door and stepped back into the fog.

Simon hurried down the attic stairs. He hooked his thumbs into his belt loops. "How do you feel, Gramps?" he asked cautiously.

"Couldn't be better!" Taking a bite of steaming oatmeal, he proclaimed, "Hospital food is for the gulls!"

"Gramps, I've got a surprise for you!" Simon ran into the shop and returned carrying his model. "I finished the battleship. I made it especially for you because we both share a deep interest in battles and history and world wars."

Gramps set the battleship in front of him. "Fine workmanship, my boy," he said. "You addressed the smallest detail with technical precision."

"I made you something too, Gramps, but it broke."

"Yeah. Josh was going to give you that kooky mouse castle," Simon said with a snicker.

Gramps raised his bushy eyebrows and glued his bulging eyes on Simon. His voice turned suddenly stern, "That castle, young man, was a creative masterpiece!"

21.

Back on Seal Island, Gramps did hip exercises, took a two-hour nap, and worked at his typewriter. Before dinner, he shaved off his prickly whiskers and changed into the tweed jacket with leather patches on the elbows. It hung off his bent shoulders as if he'd lost fifty pounds. His weathered face looked pale. Propping his walking stick by the cradle, he winced in pain as he sat down at the head of the table. Simon and Josh carried steaming red lobsters and cups of melted butter to the table. As Nana untied her apron, Gramps struggled to stand up.

"I'll do it," said Josh, quickly pulling out his grandmother's chair.

Gramps folded his hands and bowed his head. In a hoarse voice, he mumbled, "Dear Lord, bless this food set before us and the lives of all those we cherish on this good earth."

"That's the first time you've said grace in years, Hobson!" Nana reached over and gave her husband's hand a squeeze.

Simon cleared his throat. He stood up and lifted his milk glass. "I'd like to propose a toast to my grandfather's continued good health and wealth, especially after he recovers the treasure in the water cave."

Simon always knew the right thing to say to grownups. Josh pushed back his chair and lifted up his milk glass. "And I'd like to make a toast to my Nana," he said. "She's the bravest and best wife I ever met."

Nana's eyes turned misty. She raised her glass and gave a nod of thanks. "I'll miss you boys terribly," she said, blowing her nose. "Can you believe that you leave tomorrow?"

Tomorrow is finally tomorrow! Josh thought to himself. "I thought the day would never come," he grinned. Catching his grandmother's hurt expression, he said, "I mean me and Simon..." He paused. "Simon and I were afraid Gramps wouldn't get back to the island by tomorrow. We were really bummed about the accident."

"Not as bummed as I was!" Gramps chuckled. "It's been a memorable week, that is for certain!"

Simon crushed a lobster claw shell with the nut cracker. "Tell us exactly what happened, Gramps," he said, dipping the lobster meat into the melted butter. "What's it like taking off in a helicopter?"

"It was the oddest thing. I can't stop thinking about it." Gramps put down his fork and stopped chewing. "While I was lying on those rocks, I was literally paralyzed in searing pain. My hands and feet were numb with cold. Yet suddenly, I felt a great warmth surge all through my body. The pain was gone. I saw a bright white tunnel of light and I felt totally at peace. It was as if someone had lifted me out of my body. I looked down and watched myself drowning, but I felt no sense of panic or remorse. Little Jacob and our old dogs Dewey and Schooner watched with me. I was in a place I didn't want to leave."

Josh stared at his grandfather. "When I rolled you onto the floating door, you mumbled something. It sounded like, 'Don't bring me back.' Isn't that true, Simon?"

"I know what it was!" Rosie cried. "It was one of those near-death experiences. Oprah did a whole program about it on television. They even had a woman who drowned and came back to life, just like you!" Rosie chewed excitedly. "You could go on talk shows, Hobs, or even write a book about this!"

"It would be better than writing about Latin," Josh said encouragingly.

"I have no intention of discussing this experience publicly. I never even told the doctors. When I told Clemer, he said I'd lost my mind, what's left of it."

"But people would *have* to believe you, Gramps." Simon sucked more meat from the shell. "No one could make up a story like this, not unless it was true."

Gramps arched his bushy eyebrows. "This is a private matter," he said. "It need not be shared with strangers."

"But Hobs, your daughters aren't strangers. I think you should tell them everything that happened, all about the bright light and seeing Jacob and their old dogs."

"You can tell the girls whatever you like, my dear. That's why we have the cellular phone. I'm surprised you don't use it more often."

"Seriously?" Nana stared at her husband. "You've told me for years that I can't use the cell phone unless it is an emergency."

With the hint of a smile, Gramps said, "A man can change his mind! God's greatest blessing is the love of family and friends. Living on an island with an old badger like me, it's important to keep in touch with the world." Clearing his throat, he twirled the ice cubes in his whiskey glass. "The *Odyssey* leaves on the morning tide," he said. "You boys have my permission to wash the dishes. I'd advise you to pack up your things tonight before the attic gets too dark."

"I packed this afternoon," Simon said.

"I don't need to pack," Josh grinned. "I never unpacked!"

Josh washed and rinsed the huge lobster pot without wasting a drop of water. Instead of drying the dishes, Simon said he had to go to the bathroom, a trick he'd used for a month to get out of working.

Nana raised her voice above Gramps's snoring to read the final chapter of *Robinson Crusoe*. Josh made a mental note to get books on tape from the library. He could remember all the action and characters' names when someone read aloud. Walking up the attic stairs, he balanced the candle just right so that hot wax didn't drip on his fingers.

The next morning, Josh borrowed Simon's camera to finish the last roll of film. He took pictures of the house, attic, patched roof, cave, seals, eagle's nest, blueberry bushes, dock, dory, Simon in the hammock, Orton and Gillingham, the *Odyssey,* and Homer's empty birdcage. He saved two pictures to photograph his grandparents on the dock. Gramps was waiting for him in the shop when he returned.

"I'd like to have a word with you, Joshua," he said.

"If it's about the accident, Gramps, I'm really, really sorry. I meant to come help you on the dock, but..."

"Follow me," Gramps interrupted. He grabbed his walking stick and began to hobble down the path toward the woods. Instead of taking the trail to the cliff, he lead Josh to the overgrown cemetery.

"Rosie can't talk about these things," he said, pointing to a tilting, moss-covered tombstone. "She gets too emotional. I need to give you instructions about my death."

"You mean your next death," Josh said seriously.

Gramps nodded his head. "Bury my ashes exactly where I'm standing." He planted his work boots firmly on the ground. "I don't want a fancy funeral or an expensive coffin, you hear that?"

"How come you're telling me this stuff and not Simon?" Josh asked.

"You are just as capable as your brother."

Josh gave his grandfather a quizzical look. "But Simon gets an A+ in everything. I only get high marks in effort, attitude, and gym."

"Precisely my point. I've watched you boys for a month. You are a determined lad with a good many talents. With your level head, cleverness, work ethic, and sensitivity to people, you'll go just as far in life as your studious brother, mark my word."

Josh wanted to hug his grandfather. He held back, afraid of knocking him over or appearing too emotional. "Thanks, Gramps," he said. "What you just said makes me feel even prouder than when Coach Ward named me most valuable player. When I really try, I guess I'm pretty good at lots of stuff, even if I still can't spell."

Gramps nodded. "Right you are!" he said. He leaned his weight on Josh's shoulder as they walked along the cleared trail to the house.

The sun sparkled on the water as the *Odyssey* chugged past Clemer's orange and green lobster buoys. Josh never mentioned his work on the drain tide dock. Gramps would be mighty impressed at the next low tide. Simon sat quietly in the stern, reading the last chapter of his sixteenth book. Josh still hadn't read the required sixth grade reading assignment, but he'd finished lots of chapters in the *Maine Coast Marine Life* book. When he got back to school, he'd join the Environmental Club, if it didn't interfere with soccer practice. He pledged to himself to keep seals and whales and all the wildlife that lived on Seal Island safe forever.

Josh turned over his hands and looked at the calluses. He flexed the new muscles in his arms. If he could hammer shingles on a roof, chop down trees, build a dock, burn a whale, and keep control of the dory with whitecaps in the harbor, he figured he could handle sixth grade. He'd use his level head and do just fine, even if he still needed Orton and Gillingham tutoring.

"I dibs the front seat by the window on the trip home," Simon said, looking up from his book.

"How come you always get to sit in the front seat?"

"I'm the oldest, little Bro, that's why."

"You may be the oldest," Josh said slowly, "but I deserve to sit in the front seat just as much as you do!"

Simon shrugged. "Okey-dokey," he said with a puzzled expression.

Gramps turned around and offered Josh the helm. At first he hesitated. Then he stood up and gripped the wheel with both hands. Josh repeated his grandfather's string of directions under his breath. All by himself, he steered the boat around bright, bobbing lobster buoys and over the ocean swells.

"Never knew you could handle a motor boat, Joshua."

"Neither did I!" Josh grinned. In the far distance, he spotted a lone figure standing on the dock in Moxie Cove. As the boat got closer, he recognized a woman waving a red bandanna. Josh gave the helm back to his grandfather. He sat down next to his grandmother and squeezed her hand. "Thanks, Nana, for inviting us to

Seal Island," he said. "It was the worst and the best summer of my whole life!"

Josh leaned over and tapped Simon on the knee. "Our ride to New Jersey is waiting," he said, pointing to the dock.

With a confident grin, Josh took back over the helm and steered the *Odyssey* to the mainland.

About the Author:

Caroline Janover grew up in New Hampshire and spent part of every summer on her family's island in Maine. She graduated from Sarah Lawrence College and holds master's degrees in special education from Boston University and Fairleigh Dickinson University. Mrs. Janover is currently a Learning Disabilities Teacher-Consultant in the Ridgewood, NJ, public school system. Her previous books include *ZIPPER: THE KID WITH ADHD* (Woodbine House), *THE WORST SPELLER IN JR. HIGH*, and *JOSH: A BOY WITH DYSLEXIA*. Caroline Janover has dyslexia and lectures nationally with humor and insight about the creative talents and academic challenges of children who grow up with ADHD and dyslexia.